Linda Joy Singleton lives in northern California and often has strange encounters with playful cats, demanding dogs, and even pigs and horses. She has two grown children and a wonderfully supportive husband who loves to travel with her in search of unusual stories.

Linda Joy Singleton is the author of more than twenty-five books, including the series *Regeneration*, *My Sister the Ghost, Cheer Squad,* and, coming soon from Llewellyn, *The Seer.* Visit her on the Web at www.LindaJoySingleton.com.

To Write to the Author

If you'd like to contact the author, please write to her in care of Llewellyn Worldwide and we will forward your request. Both the author and publisher appreciate hearing from you. Llewellyn Worldwide cannot guarantee that every letter written to the author can be answered, but all will be forwarded. Please write to:

Linda Joy Singleton
℅ Llewellyn Worldwide
P.O. Box 64383, Dept. 0-7387-0579-9
St. Paul, MN 55164-0383, U.S.A.

Please enclose a self-addressed stamped envelope for reply, or $1.00 to cover costs. If outside U.S.A., enclose international postal reply coupon.

Oh No!
UFO!

Linda Joy Singleton

2004
Llewellyn Publications
St. Paul, Minnesota 55164-0383, U.S.A.

FIRST EDITION
First printing, 2004

Book design and editing by Megan Atwood and Andrew Karre
Cover design by Ellen L. Dahl
Cover illustration © 2003 by Mike Harper/Artworks
Interior illustration by Ellen L. Dahl

Library of Congress Cataloging-in-Publication Data
Singleton, Linda Joy.
    Oh no! UFO! / Linda Joy Singleton — 1st ed.
       p. cm. — (Strange encounters)
    Summary: While on a camping trip, Cassie Strange has a hard time convincing her skeptical parents that her sister Amber has been abducted by aliens, one of whom is doing a very good job of impersonating Amber.
    ISBN: 0-7387-0579-9
       [1. Extraterrestrial beings — Fiction. 2. Camping — Fiction. 3. Fraud — Fiction. 4. Family life — Fiction. 5. California — Fiction.] I. Title II. Series.

PZ7.S61770h 2004
[Fic] — dc22   2004040920

Llewellyn Publications
A Division of Llewellyn Worldwide, Ltd.
P.O. Box 64383, Dept. 0-7387-0579-9
St. Paul, MN 55164-0383, U.S.A.
www.llewellyn.com

Printed in the United States of America

Coming soon from Linda Joy Singleton

Strange Encounters #2: *Shamrocked!*

The Seer #1: *Don't Die, Dragonfly*

To my parents, Edwin and Nina Emburg, for
camping trips and out of this world ideas.

To a fantastic writer, Dotti Enderle, for sharing her
publisher with me.

And to my wonderful editor, Megan, for making
dreams come true.

Contents

chapter one

Roughing It

It all started with the stowaway duck.

I'd just graduated from fifth grade into summer vacation, and I was looking forward to a family campout. The Strange family (yes, that's really our last name) was hitting the road. Mom, Dad, my brother Lucas, my sister Amber, and I, were going camping at China Flat Campground.

Usually Lucas, Amber, and I stayed with our grandparents while our parents traveled around the world in search of weird happenings for Dad's job.

But not this summer.

Our green minivan was packed with sleeping bags, pillows, blankets, tents, a cooler, flashlights, and five cans of bug spray. No TV. No refrigerator. No computer games. And no hairdryer for an entire weekend.

We were really roughing it, but I didn't mind. I was thrilled. With my "strange" family, I jumped at any chance to do something so Typical American.

See, I'm the only non-strange Strange. If I were a color, I'd be medium brown, like my hair. My last teacher wrote on my report card that I was "average." Mom seemed disappointed by this, but I was relieved. It's easier being average than being noticed.

And people sure noticed my family. Dad isn't like a regular dad because he's *famous*. He looks normal enough with wavy chestnut-brown hair and friendly gray eyes. But normal fathers aren't TV celebrities. Dad has his own cable show called *I Don't Believe It!*, where once a week he proves odd happenings have logical, scientific explanations.

Mom isn't average, either. She's really into environmental causes and projects. She grows her own vegetables, flowers, and herbs. Last year, when she marched in a protest to save a two-thousand-year-old redwood tree, she wore a dress grown from grass seed. I swear I saw a worm peeking out above her knee.

And it doesn't stop with my parents. My ten-year-old brother, Lucas, wants to be an actor, so every week he transforms into a new character. Last week he was Harry Potter. Before that he was a gross werewolf. Lately he's been wearing a black cloak and saying, "I vant to suck your blood!" *Puh-leez.*

My sister, Amber, is obsessed with animals. She has angelic curly golden hair and big violet-blue eyes. We share a room and she has a zoo of stuffed animals crowded on her bed. She's okay for a first grader, except when she pretends to talk to her pets. Her quacks, mews, and barks sound really real.

So, when I heard the quacking coming from the back of our van, I figured Amber was goofing off.

"Shut up, Amber," I ordered, pushing my tangled hair from my face as I curled against a pillow. "I'm *trying* to rest."

"Okey-dokey," Amber said sweetly.

I yawned and tried to get comfortable. Lucas snored next to me, taking up three-fourths of the seat—the seat hog! I was exhausted from getting up at five in the morning, so I leaned against the window and closed my eyes. With the van gently rocking and the low murmur of conversation from my parents in the front seat, I started to drift off to sleep.

"*Quack! Quack!*"

"Amber! Cut it out!" I shouted.

"*Quack!*"

Lucas lifted his black cape off his face. "What? Huh?"

"Amber is making duck noises," I griped. "Be quiet, Amber, or I'll tell Mom."

"Don't tell. I'll be quiet."

But as Amber said "quiet" there was another quack.

4

Puzzled, I leaned over the seat—then gasped. Squatting on my sister's lap was a white creature with downy feathers and a bright orange beak— Amber's pet duck, Dribble.

"A stowaway!" I exclaimed. "Now you're in for it. Mom and Dad told you not to bring any pets. They're going to explode when they find out."

Right then Mom turned around, and I braced myself for the fireworks.

"Amber!" Mom shook her head with disbelief. "How could you! Ducks can't go camping."

"Dribble can," Amber insisted. "He's really, really smart."

"But you were told no pets."

"Sorry, Mommy."

"I'm very disappointed in you."

"Don't be mad." Amber's violet eyes filled with tears. "I just love Dribble soooo much. I couldn't leave him."

"I know, sweetie," Mom sighed. "You're soft-hearted like me."

Here we go again, I thought in disgust. If I'd disobeyed Mom, she'd still be yelling. But cute little Amber gets away with everything.

"We'll have to take Dribble home," Mom shifted in her seat to face Dad. "Jonathan, turn the van around."

"Impossible. There's no turning back now." Dad gave Mom a sharp look that I saw in the rearview mirror. "I need to find out about . . . you know what . . . I have to go to China Flat."

Dad's serious tone should have clued me in that something weird was going on. But in a few minutes everything was quiet again—even Dribble—and I was daydreaming about all the fun we'd have camping.

Of course, if I'd known what was going to happen at China Flat, I would have been too frightened to have any fun at all.

chapter two

A "Typical" Family

Highway 50 goes up and *up* and UP, leaving sizzling hot Sacramento Valley and climbing into the crisp, majestic mountains. Oak trees gave way to towering green pines, and suddenly Dad announced we were at our turn-off.

We crossed the bridge, then wound up a mountain deep into dense forest. There were no houses, cars, or traffic. I was beginning to wonder if we'd made a wrong turn when Dad rang out cheerfully, "China Flat Campground!"

I peered out the window, but only saw thick trees. We took a side road and I noticed some cars and motor homes. Through a break in the trees, a river sparkled like diamonds.

After passing through the main gate, we drove around until we found a vacant site. The few dozen campsites were spread out along a circular road. Each site had a paved strip for parking—but nothing else. And I mean NOTHING! No barbeque pits, electric outlets, or water hookups. We'd have to get water from an outdoor faucet that was pumped from a stream. And instead of modern bathrooms, we had to share an outhouse with other campers.

But I didn't mind.

"At last!" I rejoiced, flinging off my safety belt and jumping out of the crowded van.

I inhaled cool, piney air and wondered what we should do first. Go on a long hike or swim in the river? We hadn't taken a family trip like this ever, and I always envied my best friend, Rosalie, who enjoyed a lot of great family outings: boating, bike trips, and especially campouts. Rosalie said her brothers and sisters put up the tents, while her father cooked hamburgers on a grill and her mother organized the campsite.

Normal family stuff.

While Mom and Dad went to find the ranger to pay for our campsite, I called out, "Hey, Lucus! Amber!" I ran around to the back of the van and grabbed my suitcase. "Let's set up the tents."

They didn't answer.

I looked around and spotted Amber kneeling by a water faucet, making a mud puddle for her duck.

"Come help with the suitcases," I told her.

"I can't."

"Why not?"

"'Cause Dad said."

"Dad said you didn't have to unpack?" I asked skeptically.

"Not *that*." Amber wiped a mud smudge from her cheek. "Dad said Dribble is my respon— respon— my job, so I gotta take care of him."

"By making a mud puddle?"

"I'm giving him a bath 'cause his feathers are all droopy. Wanna see his new trick?"

"I'd rather see you unpack."

"Watch!" She gestured with her hand as she commanded, "Dribble, *hide*!"

The duck arched his neck and poked his head in the mud puddle. If I'd been in a better mood, I would have laughed. The only one the duck was hiding from was himself.

"Amber, stop playing and come set up camp."

"I gotta take care of Dribble."

"But I need help."

"Ask Lucas." She turned her back to me.

Little sisters! I thought angrily. *What are they good for anyway? Nothing!*

So I went after my brother and found him high on a large boulder pointing a stick at a jagged crevice.

"Lucas, ready to set up the tents?"

"Nay, fair maiden. Sir Lucas the Brave is stalking a foul dragon." He'd traded his Dracula cloak for a feathered cap and a knobby stick "sword."

"There aren't any dragons here," I told him. "Except maybe dragonflies."

"Yonder lies a formidable opponent!" He aimed his stick at a tiny creature scrambling under a rock. "Stand aside while I do battle."

"It's just a lizard."

"Lizards are a deadly breed of dragon," Lucas said gravely. "But fear not, I will protect you."

"Protect me from a backache. Help set up camp."

"Nay, fair maiden. I must keep watch on the dragon's lair. It is my honored duty to guard the kingdom."

Oh, brother! I thought as I stomped away. *Lucas is too strange even for our family! And to think he has such a high IQ he's going to be starting sixth grade with me in a few months. Major embarrassing! I'll have to pretend he's adopted.*

I hoped to find my parents at camp, but they hadn't returned yet. And Amber, leading her duck by a rope leash, was headed to the rocks where Lucas slashed imaginary dragons.

How can I enjoy my family vacation without my family? I thought unhappily. *Well, I'll just get things started myself. When everyone sees how much fun I'm having, they'll beg to join in. It's not like setting up a tent is hard . . . right?*

Wrong! I quickly found out.

I figured how to fit the poles together and poke them through the tent loops, but they stuck out all over and the nylon billowed wildly. When I tried to straighten it, the leaning tower of chaos collapsed on top of me. Once I crawled out, I discovered the problem.

No tent stakes.

Sighing, I trudged back to the van.

There the stakes were, by the cooler. Before grabbing them, I opened the cooler and helped myself to a strawberry cola. As I shut the lid, my elbow bumped against the sharp edge of Dad's briefcase. The black briefcase crashed to the ground, bursting open and scattering papers.

"Oh, no!" I cried as papers flew away on a swift breeze. I set down my soda and raced after the fly-away papers. "Come back!"

I must have looked like a demented dancer, jumping, reaching, and spinning as I chased the papers. Finally, all the papers were captured, and I brushed off dirt and pine needles. As I neatly returned them to the briefcase, I glanced around nervously, afraid Dad would show up and accuse me of snooping. His briefcase contained top-secret information for his show and he often warned us kids, "Keep out or be grounded for life."

Why did Dad bring his briefcase on our vacation? I wondered. He's not supposed to be working this weekend . . . or is he?

Then I saw the photo.

At first glance, it appeared ordinary. It was a picture of the night sky, like dark velvet sparkling with stars and a silvery slice of moon. But there was something else in the photo: a glowing banana stretched across the sky. It looked like a . . . but no, that was impossible.

I flipped over the photo and read five scrawled words:

UFO Sighting: China Flat Campground

Maybe the impossible *was* possible.

chapter three

To Believe or Not to Believe

A *UFO!* I thought in astonishment. *So that's why Dad wanted to camp at China Flat. He's investigating a UFO sighting for his TV show! But this is supposed to be my* normal *family campout!*

Unfair! I'd go right to my parents and tell them I'd had enough of strange and was moving in with Rosalie. But I couldn't stop looking at the picture. My curiosity grew like an incurable disease, making me feel like I'd die if I didn't find out what was going on.

Who had sighted the UFO? Was it a faked photo or the real thing? Probably a hoax. Dad didn't believe in anything unusual. And Mom trusted Dad's opinion. But I couldn't help but wonder if spaceships and little green men truly existed.

Running my fingers over the briefcase lid, I thought about this. Did I believe in UFOs? Logically, since people lived on this planet, they might live on other planets, too. But an idea like this was disloyal to Dad. Jonathan Strange's daughter should *not* believe in UFOs.

The last time someone reported a UFO to Dad's show, it turned out to be a faked video of a toy spaceship, and the aliens were kids in costumes. It's crazy what people would do for a million dollars—that's the prize Dad's show offered to anyone who could prove something paranormal was real. But so far no one had won the money. And once a week Dad continued to outsmart fakers in front of millions of viewers. He closed the show with his famous phrase, "And now you know why I don't believe it."

Dad was a hero, rescuing truth from liars, and I was secretly proud of him—even if his TV show was kind of lame.

But I felt no pride in my father as I stared at the photograph. Dad had lied to us about our vacation. A fun weekend in the mountains, enjoying nature, fresh air, and swimming in the river—all a lie! Dad had neglected to mention the glowing spaceship.

I won't let him get away with this, I vowed. *I'm going to confront him and demand to know the truth.*

•   •   •

I didn't get a chance to be alone with Dad until after lunch.

Our camping lunch menu was cucumber-and-apricot–jelly sandwiches, baked wheat chips, kiwi and kumquat slices, green-tomato juice. Typical Strange.

Mom had picked the fruit and vegetables from a co-op garden and canned the jelly herself. Not traditional camping food, but at least we sat around a folding picnic table like a normal family.

Unfortunately, it only lasted for twenty minutes.

Then Lucas jabbed at the air with his "sword" and scampered off on a quest for "dragons." Mom and Amber left to find the outhouse, with Dribble waddling ahead of them on his leash. And Dad began to set up the tent.

"Uh, Dad?" I cleared my throat. "We have to talk."

"We sure do, Cassie." My father knelt on the ground, long metal poles clinking as he fit them together. "You made a mess of things."

"I did?" I gulped. Had Dad found out I'd been in his briefcase?

"Hey, it's no big deal." Dad chuckled. "I'm proud you tried to assemble the tent by yourself. Everyone makes mistakes the first time."

"Oh! The tent!" I said, relieved. "Yeah, I messed up. But what I want to find out now is—"

"How to assemble a tent properly," Dad interrupted. "Just watch me, Cassie. I knew this campout would prove educational. Think of a tent as a big puzzle—"

"There's a bigger puzzle—I mean—Dad, why are we *really* at China Flat?"

"To relax and enjoy nature."

"And?" I prompted.

"To learn how to put up a tent." Dad grinned. "Watch how this pole fits into this hole. This piece connects here, then the next piece slides right in. See, nothing confusing about tents."

"But I *am* confused. I want to know the truth."

"Of course you do." Dad reached out to ruffle my hair. "So watch closely while I demonstrate. Hold the end of the pole and . . ."

Sighing, I reached for the tent pole. Dad was impossible to talk to when he slipped into his lecturing mode. Like last month when I was doing homework, and I asked him on what date the stock market crashed. Instead of simply telling me the date, he pulled out a ton of old photo albums and launched into a long story about how his great-grandfather joined a circus during the De-pression. He never did tell me the actual date. It would be easier talking to Dribble.

So I'd have to find out about the UFO another way—even if it meant spying on my own parents!

chapter four

Beware of Dogs

After a busy day of hiking, water fights with Lucas, playing hide 'n' seek with Amber and Dribble, and eating a dinner of Mom's tofu-sesame burgers, I was ready to climb into my sleeping bag and go to sleep.

But when Dad pulled out some papers from his briefcase, then whispered to Mom, I realized something was up.

Once Lucas, Amber, and Dribble were asleep, I crept out of my sleeping bag just in time to see Dad slip away from camp.

"Good luck with Mr. Lester," Mom called out with a wave. Then she yawned and retreated into their tent.

Mr. Lester? I'd never heard the name before, but I suspected he was the man who'd sent Dad the UFO picture.

This is my chance to spy! I thought.

I grabbed my jacket, then tiptoed out of my tent. A silvery moon helped me keep Dad in sight as he passed three empty campsites and a motor home. Crickets made soft noises and a river rushed on. Dad slowed as he neared the bridge, then turned into a campsite with a dented gray truck, a rusty white trailer, and a lantern glowing on a table. I hid behind a pine tree and watched Dad greet a bearded man I guessed was Mr. Lester. But it wasn't the burly man that snared my interest. It was his dogs.

Two black Doberman pinschers were poised like deadly bookends on each side of Mr. Lester. They growled and lunged toward Dad.

"Hey, call them off!" Dad jumped back, raising his briefcase like a shield.

"Brutus! Julius!" Mr. Lester ordered. "Down, you dang mutts." The dogs instantly sat, but their fur bristled and they continued to growl.

I loved dogs, especially our big clumsy rottweiler, Honey. A neighbor was watching her and our other pets while we were gone. We'd wanted to bring Honey along, but she couldn't ride in cars without barfing all over. Poor old dog was fourteen—almost one hundred in dog years. Honey slept most of the time and was so gentle she let our cat, Trixie, curl up in her tail.

But there was definitely nothing gentle about these brutes. Someone had taken cute little puppies and trained them to be attack dogs. Probably Mr. Lester.

"About time you showed up," Mr. Lester growled at Dad. "I'll only be here a few more days, then I'm moving on."

Dad smiled and gave a reply that I couldn't make out. So I crept even closer, hiding behind a large rock.

Both men faced each other across a table. A soft breeze carried Mr. Lester's words to me, ". . . ship in the sky. Glowed like a lightning bug."

"Your photograph was quite impressive," Dad remarked.

"You bet it was. I had to think fast when I saw the glowing ship, so I grabbed my camera and started taking pictures."

"Incredible," Dad said as if he were overcome with awe.

I couldn't help but grin. I recognized Dad's warm, friendly tone. Sort of like a spider smiling as he invited an unsuspecting fly into his sticky web. Dad didn't believe Mr. Lester for a minute, and as soon as he had the facts, he'd prove it on national TV.

"I figured you'd be impressed," Mr. Lester bragged. "That's why I called you, instead of your competitor, that other TV fella, whatshisname—Mooncroft."

It's more likely you're after the million dollars, I guessed. Hardly anyone took *Mooncroft's Miracles* seriously. It was a trashy cable show with wacko guests who claimed to be Elvis, or to be able to control the weather or talk to rocks.

The host of the show, Mystical Mooncroft, had been a stage magician before he started his own TV show and he was Dad's worst enemy, since Dad exposed him for conning elderly clients out of lots of money when he was a magician. After Mooncroft was almost arrested, he swore revenge on Dad.

"Of course, I'm flattered you chose me," Dad said smoothly. "On the phone, you promised to show me something unusual."

"That's right! What I got will shock the hair right off your skin." He chuckled. Mr. Lester's laugh was even creepier than his dogs' growls. "See, I was watching when it fell from the sky. At first, I thought it was one of them alien fellas. So I sent my dogs to track it down. But it weren't anything living."

"Amazing! What did you find?" Dad asked. I wasn't sure whether to gag or applaud his phony sugar-sweet tone. It was obvious that Lucas inherited his acting talent from Dad.

"I got proof that spaceships and aliens are real," Mr. Lester boasted. "Solid evidence from outer space. A glowing, gold, alien *thingamajig.*"

Wow! I thought. If this is real, it could change the world—maybe even my family.

My curiosity jumped into overdrive. I had to see more!

Cautiously, I crept toward a large pine tree, hoping to get a better look. I held my breath as I slowly moved forward. I was halfway to the tree, just a few more steps, when my foot landed on a brittle branch. *Crrraack!* The branched snapped loudly.

My heart pounded. I peered around anxiously. Dad and Mr. Lester kept on talking as if nothing unusual had happened. But the dogs perked their pointed black ears and growled. They jumped and started barking.

Then they took off running—right toward me!

chapter five

What's a Thingamajig?

I saw sharp teeth and gleaming eyes. I didn't need another warning; I started running, stumbling over a weed, picking myself up, racing to the tree. Growls rumbled behind me. Too close! I made a wild grab for a low branch and swung myself up.

Safe! I thought—until I felt a tug on my foot and looked down.

One of the dogs was eating my shoelace!

"Let go!" I screamed, clinging tightly to the branch.

I felt hot doggie breath on my ankle. I kicked out with all my strength and my shoelace snapped in half. Trembling, I leaned weakly on the branch while down below Brutus and Julius played tug-of-war with my broken shoelace.

Mr. Lester and Dad rushed forward.

"Brutus, Julius! What you got there?" Mr. Lester hollered.

"It's a kid . . . my kid!" Dad pointed up at the tree. "Cassie, is that you?"

"Uh . . . Hi, Dad." I gave a feeble wave. "Nice night, uh, for a walk. Or a climb."

"Cassie! What the devil are you doing here?"

"Trying not to get eaten alive." I looked at Mr. Lester. "Could you call off your dogs?"

"Heel. Sit!" Mr. Lester commanded gruffly. The dogs spit out my shoelace, then obediently tromped back to their master.

I let out a deep breath as I jumped to the ground.

"Cassie, you better have a good explanation for being here," Dad demanded.

"Uh, well . . ." I wrung my hands together.

"So, this is your kid, Strange?" Mr. Lester asked suspiciously.

"Yes, Mr. Lester. This is Cassandra," my father said in his smooth, confident TV personality voice. "We call her Cassie for short. She's . . ." Dad paused. "She's my oldest daughter."

I glared at Dad and clenched my fists.

Oldest? Is that all Dad could say about me? If he'd introduced Amber, he'd have said she had a wonderful way with animals. If he'd introduced Lucas, he'd have praised Lucas's dramatic acting ability. But ordinary, average, boring Cassie had no special talent. I was merely the oldest.

Mr. Lester glanced suspiciously at me as he commanded his dogs to stop growling. The dogs grew silent, but they bared their teeth as if warning me to be on guard. Message received. I did not like these dogs or their master. And I could tell Mr. Lester didn't like kids either. I'm sure if Dad hadn't been there, he'd have sicced his dogs on me.

"Cassie, you should be asleep at camp," Dad said. "Go back there and I'll join you as soon as I'm done—"

"Done doing what?"

"Business," Dad said sharply.

"Ain't no business for kids either," Mr. Lester added with a snort.

"Cassie doesn't know anything about . . . you know what."

"Good. Tell the brat to get lost so we can finish our business."

"Do *not* speak rudely to my daughter. I'll deal with her my way." Dad turned to me with a warning look. "Cassie, go to your tent."

"But Dad—"

"Now."

With a scowl, I whirled around and stomped off. Why did Dad always treat me like a baby? It was so humiliating! In two years, I'd be a teenager, almost an adult. I was old enough to handle the truth. I could be a big help to Dad if he'd just give me a chance.

Now, I'll never find out about the glowing, gold thingamajig, I thought, kicking a pinecone out of my way.

What could it be? A light reflector from a spaceship? A dangerous Martian weapon? Or a suitcase full of the latest alien fashions?

It was probably just a hoax . . . or was it?

My gaze lifted toward the night sky and I half-expected to see a banana-shaped spaceship zoom by. But I saw nothing except stars and a faint, misty moon.

Yet I had an eerie sense of not being alone—like somewhere from space, or maybe closer, someone was watching me.

chapter six

Out with Outhouses

I tossed and turned in my sleeping bag on the hard ground, trembling with dreams of evil, bug-eyed aliens chasing me. Their bony fingers were sharp knives, clawing, tangling my hair . . . until I suddenly woke up.

It's okay. It was just a dream, I told myself. My heart slowed to normal, and I began to relax—until I glanced at the sleeping bag beside mine. Dribble was curled up on Amber's pillow, but her sleeping bag was empty!

I turned on my flashlight and checked my watch. *Almost four in the morning!* So where was my sister?

Before waking my parents, I went to look for Amber.

Mountain fog had formed overnight, making it hard to see even with a flashlight. I glanced up in the sky but could barely see nearby treetops. A spaceship could be floating overhead and I wouldn't have a clue.

Shivering, I headed for the rocks where Amber had played yesterday. "Amber . . . are you here?" I called.

No answer.

I walked around a clump of manzanita trees and climbed up a large granite boulder. I shined my flashlight in a full circle and only saw a sea of misty fog.

Leaves rustled. My heart in my throat, I stared at a dark clump of bushes. Another rustle. Then a bright light struck my face.

I couldn't breathe. I couldn't move.

Was I going to be attacked by an alien?

But the next voice I heard wasn't alien at all—it was merely strange. Amber Strange, to be exact.

"Hi, Cassie," my sister said softly.

"Put that flashlight down, Amber!" I snapped. "You're hurting my eyes!"

The bright beam lowered, and I looked down from my perch on the rock. My little sister wore flannel Snoopy-patterned pajamas and her pale hair shone like white fire under the moonlight. She looked like a golden angel. Of course, my thoughts toward her at the moment were far from angelic. My heart still pounded so wildly it hurt to breathe.

I leaped to the ground and faced her with my hands on my hips. "Why did you sneak up on me?" I demanded.

"I gotta go potty."

I groaned. Just what I needed to start the day. A visit to the stinky outhouse. Every time I went there I had to plug my nose and slap away mosquitoes.

"Can't you wait?"

She shook her head.

"Mom will take you when she wakes up," I suggested hopefully.

"I gotta go. NOW."

Instead of returning to my warm sleeping bag, I was headed for an outhouse. Just great.

But when we reached the outhouse, there was a line waiting to get in. A dark-haired woman and a little girl with glasses bigger than her face shifted impatiently by the door.

"What's going on?" I asked. "Is someone in there?"

"My sister Sarah," the girl answered. "She's barfing," she added.

I frowned. "She's sick?"

"Yeah. Sarah won our prune-eating contest. She ate twenty-six and I only ate nine." The little girl rubbed her tummy. "I don't feel so good either."

"My daughters could be a while," the dark-haired woman told me, apologetically. "I hope you aren't in a hurry."

"I'm not . . . but my little sister is."

Amber danced in place. "I got to go potty . . . bad."

"Why don't you try the outhouse across the river?" the woman suggested.

"I didn't know there was another one."

"Hardly anyone uses it since it's on the other side of the river. Follow this road, cross the bridge, and then take the path on the left. You can't miss it."

"I hope not," I said uneasily.

With a sigh, I took Amber's hand and led her down the road. After we crossed the bridge, I made a left onto the path. The uneven path twisted around trees, over rocks, and far away from camp. I finally spotted the rickety wooden outhouse in a misty meadow.

While I waited for Amber, I found a log to sit on. The fog was fading to a pale mist and gray-blue sky peaked through shadowy treetops. I gazed upwards, feeling as insignificant as a tiny ant on a small planet in this vast universe.

"Face it, Cassie," I told myself, as I stared at the sky. "Dad's right. Everything has a logical explanation—even that glowing thing with those weird, blinking green lights."

"Weird, blinking green lights!" I repeated, staring ahead with horrified fascination.

I jumped up and rubbed my eyes to make sure I wasn't dreaming. But the glowing thing was real— *too real*—and it was floating in place over the grassy meadow!

Terror tingled from my scalp to my toes. Yet I was fascinated, too. This was real, and I was seeing it with my own eyes. I had to get closer, to find out if this was the UFO Mr. Lester reported. It was about the size of a school bus and all shimmery—like it was alive.

I hunched down behind low bushes. Creeping forward, I noticed two dark squares at each end of the banana-shaped thing. I tiptoed even closer, and wondered if the dark squares were doors. If so, that meant something was inside. Then a worse thought hit me. Maybe something had been inside, but it was outside now.

Outside with me.

Thoughts of bravery turned tail and fled. I raced back to the outhouse.

"Amber!" I cried frantically. "Hurry, hurry!"

She didn't answer, so I pounded on the door.

"Come out now! We have to leave right away!"

Still no answer. Forget privacy, I jerked open the door.

The flashlight Amber had been holding rolled to my feet and landed in the dirt.

The outhouse was empty.

Amber had vanished.

chapter seven

Amber-napped

"**A**mber!" I yelled desperately, the outhouse door slamming with a hollow bang.

Whirling around, I stared toward the meadow, terrified that my sister had encountered the aliens. But the strange banana-ship wasn't there. Fear choked me, and I ran forward calling Amber's name.

Where was my little sister?

Tears filled my eyes. This couldn't be happening. Amber would jump out from the bushes any minute and laugh at my silly worries. She had to be safe. She just *had* to be.

But she didn't answer my calls or pop out from the bushes. I yelled till my voice grew hoarse. I shined the flashlight in every bush near the outhouse. I have no idea how long I searched, but finally I gave up.

Amber was truly missing.

There was nothing I could do, except run to camp for help.

"Mom! Dad!" I hollered, barreling into our gloomy campsite. "Help! Someone help!"

A light flashed from within my parents' tent and there was a zip sound as the nylon wall opened. I blinked back my tears as Mom and Dad sleepily staggered out from their tent. Mom wore a long, ghostly white flannel nightgown and Dad had on a baggy red sweatshirt that didn't quite cover his striped boxer shorts.

"What is it, Cassie?" Mom rushed forward and wrapped her arms around me. "Are you all right?"

Dad snapped to alertness, looking all around. "What's wrong? Did you see a bear?"

"Not a bear! The banana ship took her!" I sobbed. "You have to help!"

"A banana ship?" Mom rubbed her sleepy eyes. "What are you talking about?"

"Slow down, Cassie," Dad said gently. "Take a deep breath and tell us what's going on."

I took a deep breath, but I was shaking so badly my teeth began to chatter. I sank down on a bench and took three more deep breaths.

"Where were you just now?" Mom asked.

"Outhouse," I managed to whisper.

"You shouldn't wander off by yourself. You're supposed to keep an eye on your sister."

"I WAS! But I saw the blinking green lights and when I went back to the outhouse it was empty!"

"Cassie, you're not making any sense," Dad said. "Why shouldn't the outhouse be empty if you weren't in it? And what's this nonsense about green lights?"

"It's not nonsense! It's real and I saw it myself, but when I went back for Amber, she wasn't there!"

Mom's hand flew to her chest. "Amber!"

"Cassie, don't upset your mother with wild tales." Dad frowned at me. "I listened to enough far-fetched stories last night, and I'm in no mood to hear more from you, too."

"It's not a story!" I insisted, clenching my fists. "It's real! I saw the green lights and banana thing and then Amber—" my voice broke off and I covered my face with my hands.

Mom pried my hands down. "What about Amber?" she demanded. "Where's my baby?"

I just cried some more. I felt so responsible and helpless. Amber was probably passing Jupiter on her way to another galaxy right now, and there was nothing I could do.

"This is ridiculous," Dad stated. "Amber is fine. She's in the tent."

"No, *no*, NO!" I shook my head. "She's been abducted by aliens!"

Mom jumped away from me and headed for the tent. Dad and I followed.

When Mom unzipped the tent and pushed aside the netted opening, we all stared inside. But I was the only one who gasped.

Amber wasn't speeding through the stars in a banana spaceship.

She was fast asleep in her own sleeping bag.

chapter eight

Going Quackers

Hours later, I was in a terrible mood. I don't know what was worse: fearing my sister had been kidnapped by aliens or making a fool of myself to my parents and discovering that Amber was safe and sound.

Either way I lose.

"Fear not, fair sister, it was but a bad dream," Lucas said as we sat at the table, buttering our cinnamon oatbran rolls. The sun was just peeking over the mountains, and we were the only ones awake.

Frowning, I took a bite of my dry roll. No camp-fire and sizzling pancakes and bacon for the Strange family. We were still a long ways from becoming typical.

"It was *not* a dream. I know the difference between real life and fantasy." I pointed at his tan cap and stick sword, and added sarcastically, "Unlike some people."

"My cap and sword are theatrical props because I am a serious actor. When I use my imagination, it's art. I know I'm me just wearing a costume. I'm not really slaying a dragon, sucking blood, or taking a ride in a spaceship."

"I never said I *rode* in a spaceship." I stomped my foot on the dirt. "But I did see a banana ship with blinking lights, and I was terrified when Amber vanished. Why won't anyone believe me?"

"Because Amber didn't vanish, fever-brained damsel. Amber came back to camp and went to sleep."

"I know . . . but it doesn't make sense."

"You're the only one not making sense. If there had been a spaceship, Amber would have seen it, too."

Lucas sounded so logical that I began to doubt myself. Had I been dreaming? But the hike to the outhouse and the blinking green lights seemed so real. And the terror I felt when Amber had vanished wasn't imagined. Hmmm. Amber. Maybe she had seen the spaceship, too. But she'd been so scared, she'd run back to camp and fallen asleep. I'd talk to her when she woke up and get to the bottom of this.

I heard a rustling and glanced over as Amber came out of our tent. Her hair was smoothed around her face like a silky blond veil, and she wore a yellow flowered sundress.

"Good morning," Amber chimed, sitting at the table. She spotted the opened bag of rolls and pounced on them. "These smell delicious. May I have one?"

Sleeping on uneven ground in a lumpy sleeping bag must really agree with Amber. She practically glowed with energy, while my head ached from dark dreams.

"Sure," I said. "But then we have to talk."

Amber took a roll, and then glanced around. "Where have the parents gone?"

"'The parents'? You playing some kind of pretend-to-be-a-grownup game?" Lucas chuckled. "*Mom and Dad* are taking a nature walk."

"Where are they going?" Amber asked in that same pretend grown-up voice.

"Maybe to visit someone," I added, thinking of Mr. Lester.

"They said they'd be back soon." Lucas glanced curiously at Amber. "Aren't you going to butter your roll?"

"Of course." Instead of using a knife to spread the butter, Amber dipped her roll into the container.

Lucas started to laugh, but I was far from amused.

"Amber, that's disgusting!" I put my hands on my hips. "Now there's cinnamon and oat flakes in the butter."

"I only did what Lucas told me," Amber said as she brought the roll to her lips. She took a large bite, chewed, then spit it out on the table. "Foul! Putrid!"

"Huh?" I stared at Amber, surprised she knew what "putrid" meant.

"My roll tastes great," Lucas said.

"Mine's fine, too." I was immediately suspicious of Lucas. A few weeks ago, he pretended to be a castaway stranded on a desert island and dug in the backyard for bugs to eat. As a joke, he hid some bugs in my jellybean jar. When I reached into the jar, I pulled out a wiggling beetle. My scream was loud enough to be heard on Mars.

"Lucas, did you mess with Amber's roll?"

"An honored knight would never inflict pain on a helpless damsel." Lucas rose and brandished his stick-sword.

"Well, something is wrong with Amber's roll and you're the only one who plays jokes."

"You wound me deeply." Lucas clutched his heart, dramatically. "I shall ignore thy cruel insult and go off on a noble quest. There are flaming dragons in need of slaying."

"I see a rotten brother in need of slaying." But he didn't hear me. He was already bounding up on a rock and jabbing at the empty air.

"Cassie, I'm not hungry anymore." Amber stood up from the table.

"Give your roll to Dribble. Your duck will eat anything."

"Dribble?" Amber glanced at the duck splashing the puddle by the campsite faucet. "Dribble is happy in the water. He does not need to eat. I'm going on a walk."

"Not by yourself, you aren't," I said, copying the forceful tone Mom uses when she wants me to do my homework. "I'm in charge of you. And I am not going to lose you again. Besides, we have to talk."

"I do not want to talk to you."

"Stop using that fake grown-up voice," I said angrily.

"You are very mean," she told me. "I just wish to walk."

"FINE!" I stormed up from the table and slipped on my sandals. "We'll go on a walk to the outhouse where you vanished last night."

"Vanished?" She scrunched her forehead. "I did not go anywhere."

"You were *gone*. And I know you had to have seen that weird spaceship. Why won't you tell Mom and Dad?"

She turned around, clearly unwilling to face me. "You were dreaming."

"How many times do I have to say it? I WAS NOT DREAMING!"

"If you insist." Amber picked up a prickly pinecone from the ground and bounced it in her hand like a ball. "Can we just walk? But not to the outhouse. I want to see the campground."

"Okay." I fought to keep my temper. "We'll walk around and if we find Mom and Dad, you're staying with them. I'm sick of being your babysitter."

"I don't need sitting."

"Yeah, right." I scowled. "Put your leash on your duck so we can go."

"Dribble can stay here."

"Are you kidding? After the stink you made by bringing that dumb duck on our campout, now you want to leave him behind?"

"You're right." Her smile oozed sweetness. "I was kidding. Here, Dribble. Let's go."

Amber reached for Dribble, but the duck quacked a protest.

"Come here, Dribble."

"Quack, *quack,* QUACK!" Feathers fluttered as Dribble waddled away.

"What's with your duck?" I asked.

"He's playing a game." Amber lunged for the duck, only he dodged and quacked, waddling faster. He made a full circle around the camp, coming over to hide behind me.

But what was he hiding from?

chapter nine

Bubble, Bubble, Potato Trouble

"Dribble, stop playing hide 'n' seek," Amber ordered. "You're a naughty, naughty boy."

"Your duck is so dense." Bending down, I scooped up the feathered fuzz-brain. I started to hand him to Amber, but she shook her head.

"Dribble has been bad, so he is grounded. Bad ducks do not go on walks."

"Whatever." I found a rope and tied Dribble to the water faucet. When I turned back to Amber, she was gone.

Not again!

"I'm going to strangle that little brat," I muttered.

I was in no mood for a game of hide 'n' seek. But I didn't have much choice so I looked in my tent, Mom and Dad's tent, and the van. No Amber.

Walking over to the dirt road, I peered in the distance and saw a flash of white and blue. That sneak! Amber was taking off by herself.

It was tempting to just let Amber go. Good riddance! If she got lost or eaten by a bear, then she'd be sorry. Of course, if anything really did happen to her, Mom and Dad would blame me.

So I started running up the road. Dusty red dirt kicked up around my sneakers as I passed tents, campers, and motor homes. I noticed a TV antenna on a luxury motor home and ached with envy. It was only my second day of roughing it, and I already missed the comforts of electricity. What I wouldn't give for a remote control and a big-screen TV.

"Amber!" I called as I reached a fork in the road.

Small wooden signs pointed to numbered camp-sites, but I had no idea which direction Amber had taken: left, right, or straight. I went left across a small bridge, but when I reached a dead end, I knew left was wrong, so I doubled back and took the right path.

This road went on forever, curving this way and that, until finally I realized I'd gone in a complete circle. So the only way to go was straight ahead. The road narrowed and grew rocky, turning into a rough hiking path. I was tired and out of breath. I wanted to turn back—until I saw a flash of blue through a patch of wild berries.

Amber! Sighing with relief, I hopped over a ditch after my sister. As I drew closer, I opened my mouth to call for her, then changed my mind. What was Amber doing?

Quietly, I peered through some bushes at my sister. She sat on a log, cradling something small and gray on her lap.

"*Gwik nekawaka broteeni.*" Amber spoke strange words I couldn't understand. But that wasn't unusual. Amber was always talking to her pets in made-up languages. Was the gray thing on her lap a wild bird or squirrel?

I crept closer, my curiosity mounting.

Amber's hands were cupped together and she murmured more odd words. The gray object in her lap wasn't alive. It looked like a plastic toy potato.

Then an incredible thing happened.

Amber brought the "potato" up to her lips and *kissed it!*

Suddenly, little pink bubbles whooshed out of the potato toy. They swirled like a pink cloud over Amber's head. Dozens, hundreds, a whole army of cotton-candy bubbles.

The bubbles danced on a breeze. Each bubble ballooned to the size of a baseball. I stared at three that floated near my face. Then, I reached out to pop one. Only it didn't pop. It clung to my finger like it was made of glue, swelling bigger and bigger, surrounding my fingers and my hand.

"LET GO!" With my free hand, I pushed it away, but it grabbed that hand, too. Backing up, I waved my arms, trying to break free. Only now the bubble was the size of a door. And it sucked me inside like a vacuum, slurping my arms, my hips, my head . . .

The hungry pink bubble swallowed my whole body!

chapter ten

Splash Attack

I confess, I freaked out.

"Amber!" I screamed, hitting and kicking my pink prison. "Help! Help!"

"Cassie?"

Amber peeked through the bushes and gaped at me. "What are you doing with my bubble?"

"It swallowed me! Get me out of here!"

Amber frowned, then muttered something under her breath.

Pop, pop, pop! Pink bubble firecrackers exploded. There was a deafening *POP* and the humongous bubble surrounding me vanished. Other bubbles popped and vanished, too.

Incredible!

"I'm free!" Jumping, I waved my arms. "I don't know how you did it, Amber, but thanks. What is that thing?"

"You have interfered and ruined everything." Amber glared at me—like I was the one who'd done something wrong. "The *najlem* will not work now."

"The what? How'd you make those bubbles? Can I try it?" I reached for the potato-thing, but Amber jerked her hands behind her back. When she showed her hands again, they were empty. I blinked, feeling like I was going crazy.

"What's going on?" I demanded. "Why did you ditch me and how did you make those weird bubbles? I mean, I was trapped inside a monster bubble!"

"I did nothing." Her violet-blue eyes shone with innocence.

"What's the toy potato?"

"I do not know what you're talking about."

"I saw it. Where did it go?" I looked behind her on the ground but saw nothing but dirt. And her shorts didn't have any pockets. "Amber, this is not funny. What were those weird words you were saying? What's a najlem?"

"A pretend word for my game." She folded her arms across her chest. "I am tired of playing. I am going back to camp."

"But you haven't explained *anything!*" I objected. "Amber you've been acting weird since last night . . . weirder than usual anyway. You disappeared from the outhouse and then pretended nothing happened. But I saw a spaceship and you must have seen it, too."

"You were dreaming."

"I was not!" I sank on the log, weary and confused. My headache throbbed worse than ever.

"Poor Cassie." Amber smiled sadly. "I am sorry you had a bad, bad dream and I am sorry I ran from you. Really, I didn't see a spaceship."

I heard her words, and they sounded sincere. But deep down in my gut, I knew better.

My little sister was lying.

• • •

When we returned to camp, Mom and Dad were sitting at the table, talking in low, tense voices.

"—lowdown, rotten scoundrel," I heard Dad complain.

"Another fake?" Mom gave Dad's arm a comforting pat.

"I never found out." Dad rubbed his forehead. "He wants the million up front. Of course I refused. Then he turned nasty and made some threats."

"He can't threaten you!" Mom cried. "What are you going to—"

Mom stopped talking when she saw Amber and me.

"Hi, girls. Have a pleasant walk?" Mom asked.

"NO!" I said at the same time Amber answered, "It was fun!"

"Good, good," Dad said, standing and giving Mom a look.

Something was up with my parents and I wanted to know what. Was creepy Mr. Lester the "rotten scoundrel" threatening Dad?

"How was *your* hike?" I looked at my father curiously. "Did you meet any other campers?"

"A few." Dad took a sip from his root beer can.

"That mean man with the dogs?" I asked.

"Mr. Lester sounds like a terrible person," Mom said with a shudder. "How can he expect us to . . ." Mom's voice trailed off when Dad shook his head firmly.

"Cassie, I don't know what you heard last night at Mr. Lester's camp, but I want you to forget it."

"I can't." I pursed my lips. "This was supposed to be our family vacation—not a UFO hunt."

Mom laid a calming hand on my shoulder. "It *is* a family vacation, honey."

"UFO hunt?" Amber's eyes grew wide. "Really?"

"Of course not," Mom assured. "Cassie, that imagination of yours is running wild again. We'll do something fun as a family, soon: play a game, make crafts, or cool off in the river. We're here to enjoy nature together."

"Then why did Dad meet secretly with Mr. Lester?"

Mom shot an uneasy glance at Dad.

"My business does *not* concern you, Cassie." Dad wagged his finger at me. "No more eavesdropping. And stay away from Mr. Lester. His dogs are dangerous, and so is he."

"I like doggies," Amber put in.

"Not these doggies," I said with a shudder. Then, because I was angrier with Dad than Amber, I grabbed my sister's hand and said we were going to go swimming. Lucas was already down at the river wading in a shallow pool bordered by large rocks.

"I don't want to swim," Amber whined.

"Why not?" I stood on a granite boulder at the edge of the river and admired the rippling ribbon of clear, sparkling water. "You love splashing with your duck."

"Amber, the water's great. Come on in," Lucas said as he waded up to his knees. Quacking joyfully, Dribble swam circles around him.

"You cannot make me," Amber said stubbornly. She sat on the boulder and folded her arms across her thin chest.

"Okay." I pulled off my shirt. I was wearing my favorite black-and-white, polka-dotted swimming suit. "Lucas, Dribble, and I will have fun without you."

"I am going back to camp." Amber started to get up, but I grabbed her arm.

"You are *not* running off without me again." I narrowed my gaze at my little sister. "You'll either wade with us or sit right there until we're done. Understand?"

"Oh . . . all right."

"Cassie, you sound just like Mom." Lucas scrunched his face in mock seriousness. "'Sit right there until we're done. Understand?'" He copied my voice exactly.

"Understand THIS!" I swooped down and swept my arm across the water so that a wave splashed all over my brother.

"You ruined my hair. I had it parted and smoothed down so I'd look like a knight."

"Now you look like a knight caught in a storm," I joked. "A stormy knight."

"I'll get you!" He scooped up water, then flung it in my face. "Now who's all wet?"

Water filled my eyes and my nose. Sneezing and sputtering, I pushed my soggy hair from my face. Then I jumped into the river after my brother.

"Payback time!" I cried. "You are so dead!"

"Stop fighting!" Amber begged from a safe distance away on the shore.

But Lucas ignored her and taunted. "Come and get me!"

"Oh, I will! And when I do, you are going to be so sorry!"

Lucas just laughed. So I bent down and dove at him suddenly—the water was cold but I didn't care.

Just before I could grab his ankles and pull him under, though, Lucas dodged me by scrambling up on a large rock.

I stood up and shook the water out of my eyes. "You little chicken. Afraid of a little water?" I said.

Then, before I knew what was happening, he sprang off his rock, high into the air—"Cannonball!"—and splashed down, making a huge wave.

When the water cleared, I wasn't the only one soaked. Dribble squawked a soggy protest and flapped his dripping feathers. Then he flew onto a large boulder on the opposite side of the river.

"Did you see that, Amber?" I turned toward my sister, who sulked on the riverbank with her arms folded across her chest. "Lucas tried to drown your duck. Come on! Jump in and help me clobber Lucas!"

She shook her head. "No."

"Don't be such a baby," I told her. "The water's cold at first, but you'll get used to it. It's great."

"I don't want to go in."

"Have it your way." Lucas chuckled wickedly. "If you won't come in the river, we'll bring it to YOU!"

He dipped his cap into the water and threw a capful of water at Amber.

Direct hit!

"*Noooo!*" Amber shook her soggy blond hair.

Lucas laughed so hard, he slipped on the smooth riverbed and fell backwards; another big splash and even more laughter.

I was laughing, too, doubled over with tears streaming down my cheeks. Now this was fun! Wait till I told Rosalie. She'd never believe the Stranges had a water fight.

"Good one, Lucas!" I pushed my wet bangs from my eyes and turned to Amber. She was still shaking her hair and slapping the water on her skin as if it were poisonous.

"No, no, no!" Amber wailed. "Why did you do this to me?"

"Stop blubbering like a two-year-old and just jump in. The water's wonderful!"

"It is vile!" she shrieked. "I am leaving!"

"Running back to camp to tattle on us?" I asked sarcastically. It was hard to know what was worse: a little brother or a little sister. Right now, the Major Pain in the Rear Award went to my little sister.

"I am wet!" Amber swatted herself as if being attacked by a swam of invisible mosquitoes. "My skin will *yakalrev!*"

"Yaka– *what?*" I stepped onto the sandy shore and stared at Amber. Something about her looked and sounded . . . odd.

I shivered, but there was no wind. A deep, awful chill invaded me. Amber's hair should be dark blond with dampness, but instead it shimmered like silver tinsel. And there were blotchy patches on her face—like ugly, blue bruises.

"Your . . . your skin!" I pointed in shock, fear, and disbelief.

Amber whirled around with a shrick and ran away.

At that moment I knew the truth: Amber wasn't Amber anymore. She'd changed into a USO.

An Unidentified *Sister* Object.

chapter eleven

I Smell a Dirty Space Brat

Five odd facts all added up.

1. Amber's mysterious vanishing act, followed by her reappearance in her tent
2. The way Dribble avoided Amber instead of following her
3. Those weird words Amber used, like yakalrev
4. Pink bubbles coming from the potato-thing
5. Amber's weird reaction to water

If Amber had really been zapped into an alien, how could I rescue her? Where was the *real* Amber? Was she asleep in her own body while an alien masqueraded as her? Or was she being held captive in a spaceship suffering horrible tortures?

I imagined Amber trapped in a large glass test tube and ogled by creatures with eyes for ears and lips for eyebrows. Their creepy twenty-fingered hands would touch Amber's white-blond hair. They would wonder if all Earthlings had pale hair and violet-blue eyes. I sure hoped those aliens weren't into sharp needles or dissection.

Horrors!

I hopped some rocks, heading toward camp. There was only one thing I could do: tell Mom and Dad. I had to convince them that the banana ship had been real and this Amber was not real. My parents were smart—they'd know what to do.

But would they believe me?

Not in a zillion years.

I stopped under a pine tree. Dry pine needles crunched under my feet as I sank wearily to the ground. Mom and Dad already complained that my imagination was out of control. Even loony Lucas thought I'd dreamed the banana spaceship. And *I* wasn't even sure what to believe.

The fake Amber had fooled everyone—well, almost everyone.

Two of us were onto her deceitful alien game.

Me and Dribble.

How could an almost-sixth grader and a duck battle alien forces?

chapter twelve
Nature, Yikes!

When I stepped into our camp, Amber was there. Talk about a shocker! And Amber looked normal. (Well, as normal as an alien possessing an Earth girl's body can look.) Her face was creamy flesh again, not creepy monster blue.

Even weirder, though, was that Amber sat in a lawn chair beside my mother, weaving strips of straw into a basket.

Geez!

Mom was always trying to get us kids to "explore the environment by creating natural crafts." I was all thumbs and no artistic talent. The log cabin quilt I'd sewn for Mom's birthday was a lumpy, crooked disaster. When I made a scrapbook with pictures from Dad's TV show, I smeared glue on Dad's face in one picture and cut off his leg in another. Still, I kept hoping to find my own special talent, so I tried new things—unlike Amber. She grew bored easily and would rather be outdoors playing with her animals.

Only Amber wasn't Amber.

Which meant the alien was lame enough to weave baskets. Mom's powers of persuasion were galaxy-wide.

"Cassie, you're just in time for crafts," Mom said, tipping up her sunglasses to look at me.

"Not now, Mom."

"Sit down and make a basket."

It was more order than invitation, so I sat a wary distance from Alien-Amber and asked Mom how to start.

"Weave the strands like this." Mom twisted a long, flat straw ribbon in and out at lightning speed. "Your sister picked it up quickly. I'm delighted she's trying new experiences."

"Everything is a new experience for her."

Amber gave me a sly look. "I like to learn nature crafts."

"You already know about crafts. *Space*crafts."

"Cassie, are you still obsessing over that bad dream?" Mom asked, knitting her brows together with concern. "Do you want to discuss it?"

"Yes." I glanced anxiously at Amber. "But not here. Mom, can we talk in private? It's life-or-death important."

"Cassie, you're acting as dramatic as your brother."

"I'm not acting; this is real life." I clenched my fists at my sides. "Can we go somewhere alone?"

"How can you get more alone than this?" Mom cupped her hand to her ear. "Listen to the wind whooshing through the trees and whispering a welcome. The river rushes on like a lovely lullaby, as if we're the only people in the universe."

"But we aren't! There are others closer than you think." I shot an anxious look at Alien-Amber. "I can't just sit around weaving baskets."

"So decorate a pinecone, instead," Mom suggested. "I have glitter, colored beads, and glue. A pretty pinecone will make a lovely decoration for your bedroom."

As if that would entice me. "If you don't listen to me, I may never see my bedroom again! They may come for *me* next!"

"Who's coming?" Mom looked around curiously. "Did you make some friends at camp? Well, invite them over. I brought plenty of craft materials."

"Mom! I haven't made any new friends."

"Not yet," Amber said with a wicked smirk and gleam in her blue eyes. "Maybe later."

I trembled. *Was that a threat?*

"Cassie, relax and have fun with us," Mom said. "If you're still upset over that bad dream, relax with some yoga breathing. Deep in and blow out slowly—that always helps me focus."

"MOTHER!" I gritted my teeth. "You. Do. Not. Understand!"

"How can I understand when you're not making any sense? I'm getting tired of your melodrama, young lady. Either stay with us or play in the river with your brother."

"Want a pinecone?" Amber offered sweetly.

"I don't want anything from *you!*" I told my alien sister.

"Cassandra Lynnelle Strange! I've had enough of your attitude," Mom snapped. "There's no reason to treat your sister so rudely."

"She's not my—"

"Pinecones!" Amber interrupted. "Pinecones are very delicious." She brought a prickly cone to her mouth and took a big bite.

Crunch, crunch. Chew, chew. And *swallow.*

"Gross!" I cried. "Mom, look at her! Can't you see she's not herself? She's eating something from a *tree!*"

"Bananas, apples, and pears come from trees," Mom said.

"But *normal* people don't eat pinecones."

"Of course, they do. Nature offers us many tasty treats." Mom picked up a pinecone and pulled it apart to reveal seeds. Then she popped a seed into her mouth. "Hmmm . . . not bad. Amber, the seeds are the best part. You should spit out the rest."

"Yes, Mom." Amber took another bite and spit out a soggy clump of dark-brown cone. "That was yummy."

"Disgusting," I said with a grimace.

Amber grinned. "Try it, sis."

"No way. I only eat human food, unlike you."

"You can also eat certain flowers and plants," Mom told us, clearly pleased we were interested in learning. "We'll go on a hike later, and I'll teach you about nature's edible plate."

"Edible plate?" I shook my head. "Don't tell Amber plates are edible, or she'll start eating them, too."

Amber giggled. "People do not eat plates."

"I hope not." I gave her a wary look. She sure sounded like Amber. Without the blue blotches and silvery hair, she looked like Amber. Okay, she was acting oddly, but strange was normal in my family. Maybe I was the crazy one.

Or maybe I wasn't.

I had seen the spaceship and the pink bubbles, and I had heard Amber speak in another language—and I had seen her face and hair change. This *couldn't* be the real Amber.

Mom may not believe me, but I had to believe in myself.

And I *had* to rescue my little sister . . . even if it meant risking my own life.

chapter thirteen

Impossible Imposter

Dad popped back in at noon for a quick sandwich. His cell phone poked out of his pocket and he carried his briefcase. I knew he was on the job for *I Don't Believe It!* But when I asked him about Mr. Lester and the UFO picture, he refused to answer.

After Dad left, Mom arranged prickly weeds in her woven basket as a table decoration, and then she prepared lunch.

"Bring the zucchini bread from the cooler, Cassie," Mom said as she dug into a paper bag for heavy-duty plastic plates and silverware. No disposable utensils for my Mom. Everything would be rinsed, recycled, and re-used.

I was about to respond, when Amber offered, "I'll get it for you, Mom. Zucchini bread is my favorite."

I lowered the *National Geographic* magazine I'd been pretending to read and studied Amber as she walked over toward the car. She appeared normal, but I knew better. The real Amber's favorite dessert was strawberry shortcake. Alien-Amber probably didn't even know what a zucchini was—the fake.

All during lunch, I watched Amber.

And she knew it.

She put on a magnificent performance. She ate her entire s.l.o.p. sandwich: *s*prouts, *l*ettuce, *o*lives, and *p*ickles on zucchini bread. She even laughed at Lucas's lame jokes. And she was very helpful to Mom.

The real Amber wasn't *this* perfect.

But do you think Mom noticed?

After lunch, Amber offered to carry the recycling bag to the big Dumpster.

"How thoughtful," Mom gushed, giving Amber a hug. "You're such a good girl."

"Good something," I murmured.

Mom shot me a cold look. "Cassie, you could learn from your sister."

"Oh, I hope to learn a lot." To myself, I added, like where the real Amber is imprisoned and how to get rid of an annoying alien fake.

"And I will learn from you, too." Amber flashed a sly grin that gave me the creeps.

After she left camp with a bulky plastic trash bag, I put my plan into action. Alien-Amber seemed to be way too smart to reveal herself in front of my family, and they'd never take my word alone that she was an alien. My only hope was to follow her and find out exactly what she'd done with my real sister.

"I'm going to the outhouse." I said as I jumped up from from my chair.

"Not so fast, young lady."

I stopped in my tracks and groaned. Mom was using her I'm-going-to-make-you-work-your-fanny-off tone.

"No running off till you do your chores. You can wash the dishes and Lucas can dry." She pointed to a large pot. "Fill that pot with water from the faucet and add some organic soap."

"Can't it wait till I get back? I really have to go." I pressed my legs together. "It's not *natural* to hold it in."

"Well . . ." Mom hesitated.

I hopped in a circle and tried to appear distressed. "I need to go—SOON!"

"Oh, okay. But don't take too long."

"I won't!"

I practically flew out of the camp. Behind me, I heard Mom asking Lucas if he wanted to weave a basket.

Spotting Amber wasn't hard this time. I found her at a Dumpster, tossing the bag in, just like she said.

Amber reached up to touch her face like she was checking for zits. Scowling, she held out her hands to look at them. Something blue shimmered on her fingertips.

As I watched in stunned fascination, the tip of Amber's nose wiggled, waggled, and then *fell off*. *Plop*, straight to the ground. A silvery-blue hole glowed from in the middle of her face.

"Yakalrev!" Amber started running.

And I took off after her, crossing the paved road and taking a rough, woodsy trail.

But when I turned a corner, she was gone.

"Darn! How can she move so fast?"

Looking around, I saw no one, just a landscape of rocks, weeds, and forest. In the distance, I could hear the rushing river. The campground was far behind me and in front the path grew steep and rocky, as it curved up the mountain.

Something shiny on the ground caught my eye.

Bending over, I stared curiously at a small, creamy blob that shimmered blue in the sunlight. It was about the size, color, and shape of an ear.

I reached out slowly with my index finger and touched it.

Then I screamed.

It *was* an ear.

A *human* ear.

chapter fourteen

Ear We
Go Again

"Don't panic," I told myself. "It's just an ear. Ears don't attack people."

Still, I backed away, and checked my hand. The place where my fingertip had touched the ear glowed blue. The blue spot was smooth and tingled. I tried to rub the blue off but couldn't. And it continued to glow.

Way too creepy.

I wanted to run back to camp, show my parents my finger, and then beg them to pack up and drive home immediately. But even if they believed me (unlikely), they would never leave without Amber.

Amber! My heart ached as I stared at my shiny fingertip. *Where are you? What's happened?*

I just had to stay calm and get to the bottom of this. If I panicked, I'd never find my real sister. And the only way to find her was to stay close to her double. Alien-Amber was losing skin—even an entire ear. "Yakalrev," she called it. A flaking alien should be easy to find. Like Hansel and Gretel leaving a trail of breadcrumbs, Alien-Amber was leaving a trail of body parts. Gross, but useful.

All I had to do was follow the trail of alien skin.

About twelve feet away, I spotted another shimmer of blue on a manzanita branch. Bingo! The fragment of fallen skin still glowed bright. Amber couldn't be too far ahead.

As I passed the manzanita bush, I was careful not to touch the piece of alien flesh. I followed the blue path further up the mountain trail. By a tree trunk to my left, I saw something blue, only it turned out to be a wildflower. I compared the shades of blue from the flower and my fingertip. My finger shined a deeper sapphire-blue.

I crossed a bridge and kept walking. It seemed like miles and years, yet it was probably less than one mile and no longer than twenty minutes. My heart thumped from fear. I wanted to find Amber yet I was terrified of what I would find.

When I saw a crude wooden building, I knew exactly where I was.

The trail had circled back to the outhouse where Amber had vanished.

And there was Alien-Amber! She hurried across the grassy meadow, her skin flaking off like a bad case of dandruff.

I hid behind a tree. She didn't look like my sister anymore. She had morphed into a horrifying half human, half neon-blue creature.

The creature stopped walking and stood in the center of the meadow. She moved her lips as if muttering to herself. She kept talking, probably in some weird alien language, then rubbed her decomposing face and looked down at the ground.

What was she doing? The grassy meadow was still; there wasn't even a breeze to stir the grass. All insects probably dove for cover the moment Alien-Amber appeared.

Puzzled, I watched as the alien held out her hands and there was that potato-thing again. She brought it to her luminous blue lips and instantly the swarm of bubbles reappeared. Pink bubbles. This time there were thousands, millions, billions, *gadzillions* of them!

The bubbles billowed over Alien-Amber like a cotton-candy cloud. They swirled high over the meadow, spinning like jeweled rings. Faster and faster, until they blended together. Bubble colors changed, from pink to red to white and then to green. Suddenly they were no longer bubbles, but had transformed into an oblong bus-sized craft with flashing green lights.

The banana spaceship!

Like before, it hovered over the meadow.

One of the squares at the end of the ship slid open like a door, and Alien-Amber stepped toward it.

Ohmygosh! She was going inside the spaceship. She might zoom away to another galaxy, and I'd still be huddled here behind a tree, too afraid to save my own sister.

Memories raced through my mind. Amber and I playing monkeys jumping on our bed, then giggling when the bedsprings broke and we crashed. Amber smiling as she held out the tiny duck she'd rescued from a drainage ditch. "I'm going to call him Dribble," she'd said. Another time she'd convinced Lucas and I to put on a pet talent show for our parents. Our dog Honey wouldn't roll over for me, so I'd rolled over instead and everyone cracked up.

Amber may be annoying sometimes, but she was my sister and I wouldn't let an alien kidnap her without a fight.

"Amber!" I shrieked. Then my legs were moving, racing forward, headed for the spaceship. "Don't go!"

Alien-Amber whirled around.

Her face was horrifying: a blotchy mix of neon-blue and flaky human flesh. Her human violet-blue eye blinked while the other eye was a black hole.

"Cassie?" she exclaimed in my sister's voice. "What are you doing here?"

"You know." I clutched my trembling hands together.

"You do not belong here. Leave now."

"Not without my sister. My *real* sister."

"That's not possible." She had switched to an older voice that was alien to me. "Go before it is too late."

"I'm not going anywhere." I dug my heels into the grassy ground and gulped. Sounding brave was one thing, but inside I was Jell-O—shaking, quaking, Jell-O.

Alien-Amber shook her head, causing a chunk of her hair to fall off onto scraggly weeds.

"Your hair!" I pointed with a gasp. "It's silver."

"Of course. I take after my mother."

"Your mother . . . ?" My head spun. I was talking to Amber, and yet she wasn't Amber. An alien. A real blue-skinned, silver-haired alien. And her mother had silver hair, too.

"Cassie, I wish you had not followed me," Alien-Amber said with a sigh.

"Wh— Why?"

"Because I really like you." The alien peeled off the creamy skin off her right elbow and flicked it away. "But now you know too much."

"I don't know anything! Who are you? Where are you from? What are you doing here? What kind of weird spaceship is that?" My mind was overflowing with questions; my curiosity was in overdrive.

"That is my *rebotco* . . . like an Earth motor home. All the kids have them where I'm from." She frowned. "You ask too many questions."

"I have to know what happened to my sister," I begged. "Where is she?"

Alien-Amber shrugged. "Not far."

"Then give her back. Please!"

"I cannot." Her tone was grave.

"Why not? She's just a little girl. She never hurt anyone! Sure, once she put my favorite underwear on her duck and the stains wouldn't wash out. Then another time her pet mouse had babies on my pillow—while I was sleeping on it. But she's an okay sister." My voice broke. "I want her back . . . *please!*"

"It is too late. You are a danger to my mission." The alien took a step toward me.

"*Me?*" I took a step back. "Dangerous?"

"Yes. Very." She gave me a dark, disturbing stare. "There is only one thing I can do."

"There is?" I swallowed. "What?"

"Take you there," she paused and pointed at the banana ship, "inside my rebotco. Cassie, follow me."

chapter fifteen

Mind Into Matter

I knew it was a dumb move to follow an alien. I could end up being space-napped and never see Earth or my family again. But if Amber was on the banana ship, then I had to go there, too. Besides, it would be cool to see the inside of a real spaceship.

"Do not be afraid," Alien-Amber told me.

"Too late," I said more afraid than I'd ever been in my life. But I was determined to find Amber.

The alien tugged on my hand and pulled me through the doorway. *Whoosh!* The door automatically slid shut behind me. I heard a mechanical fizzing noise and two sharp beeps. A yellow beam flashed over my head like a spotlight. I was being showered with sunny warmth that made me feel tingly all over.

There were two more sharp beeps and a rattling noise. Turning sideways, I saw a curving, narrow plastic tube that ran from the top of the door to a chrome basket on the floor. *Rattle, rattle,* and *plink!* A white marble shot out like a high-powered spitball, joining a pile of multicolored marbles in the basket.

"Look!" With a gleeful cry, Alien-Amber swooped over and plucked the white marble from the basket. "Your *doodlezapp* is clear white. That means you are very curious and perceptive."

"*Doodlezapp?* What's that?"

"Your brain." She twirled the marble in her hand.

"My . . . *My brain!*" My hands flew to my head, checking for exit holes. But everything felt solid.

She grinned. "Not your actual brain."

"That's a relief . . . I think."

"For a human, you are really funny." She seemed to have a bigger sense of humor than the real Amber. "A doodlezapp is a copy. Like when you copy a song or movie to replay later."

"You copied my brain?" I asked incredulously.

"Sure. It is easy to do."

"But why is mine so . . . so tiny?" I pointed to a golfball-sized, ruby-red marble in the basket. "The bright red one is twice as large."

"Of course. It's from a mosquito."

"A MOSQUITO!"

"Yes. Very advanced cerebral matter."

"A mosquito has a bigger brain than I do?" I asked, outraged. "That's not fair."

"Cassie, you are hilarious!" Alien-Amber laughed. "I cannot believe you have brain envy!"

"Do not. And I don't see what's so funny." Frowning, I pointed at the basket. "Why do you copy brains, anyway?"

"It is an educational requirement."

"Homework?"

"Yes, homework. And an assignment that is so boring the shine will fade out of my hair before I'm done." She fluffed the half of her hair that gleamed silver. "My teacher is such a *dwiggwump*. He's always on my case and says I have a bad work attitude."

"I know what that's like." I nodded. "My teachers complain I daydream too much. But you're a powerful alien. You can zoom around the universe and change your appearance. Why waste your time with homework?"

"Tell that to my dwiggwump teacher!" She tossed my "brain" marble into the basket. "At least I've figured out a way to have fun with the doodlezapps."

"Fun? With brain copies?"

"Sure! Wanna play a game of marbles?" She grinned mischievously. "Doodlezapps are great for shooting marbles."

I should have been more freaked out. Panicked and terrified. Instead I was laughing . . . and it felt good. Maybe I *had* lost my marbles.

But if I had lost them, my curiosity hadn't gone with them. As I looked around Alien-Amber's spaceship, a thousand questions were fighting their way to the front of my brain.

"Why is your spaceship shaped like a banana?" I asked.

"It's simple, actually. All of our crafts are shaped like fruit, so if any humans take pictures of them, no one would believe the pictures are real. Who would think aliens would ride in bananas?"

I nodded. "In a weird way, it makes sense."

Then I grew serious as I remembered my sister. I glanced around, looking at a curved table dotted with blinking green buttons and a puffy white couch floating inches off the floor. Narrow glass shelves were inlaid into a wall and contained odd test tubes and jars oozing with ink-black liquid.

And attached to the ceiling was a narrow bed covered in a plush pink comforter. It looked like an ordinary bed—except that it hung upside down from the ceiling.

But there was no sign of Amber.

"Where is she?" I asked. "You said my sister was nearby."

"She is safe in a hidden room." Alien-Amber scratched her blotchy neck. "But I am falling apart and need to fix my skin. You almost ruined everything by getting me wet."

"The real Amber loves water."

"Water is so disgusting. Wet, slippery, and drippy. And to think you drink it!" More fake flesh flaked off as she shuddered. "I don't know how you Earthlings live in these itchy bodies."

"Human skin is better than your sticky, space-blue body." I held out my fingertip, which still glowed a bright blue. "Why won't this stuff rub off?"

"It will fade in a few days." She pointed to one of the reclining chairs. "Sit down while I repair myself."

Except for the fact that it was floating about eight inches off the ground, the couch looked fairly harmless, so I sat. I watched as Alien-Amber picked up a gold bottle and sprayed her body from head to toe. Blue skin and silver hair disappeared. Like magic, she turned back into Amber. She rummaged in a cabinet, then popped in a bright violet-blue eye.

"WOW!" I exclaimed. "If I didn't know better, I'd think I was looking at my sister."

"I am the image of Amber. My true name is Veltura. My friends call me Vee."

"Is that what I should call you?"

"Unfortunately, you will not get the chance." Vee gave a soft sigh. "This has been fun, but I am running out of time. I regret what I have to do."

"Wh— What do you mean?" I bit my lip. "I thought we were having fun . . . becoming friends."

"Friends?" she asked, puzzled.

"Yeah. Sure, we're a little different, but we were having fun at camp and now I've seen your spaceship. You wouldn't do anything to a friend. Would you?"

"I don't want to. But it's not my choice." Vee sighed. "I envy the real Amber. She is lucky to have a sister like you."

"Let me see my sister so I know she's safe." Panicked, I whipped my head around, wondering where the secret room was hidden.

"She is completely safe and happy."

"Happy? Alone in an alien prison?"

"Did I say she was alone? No, I did not. She is playing with pets from other planets: baby *goofinks*, bearded *snogards*, and a winged *katahsie*."

"Let us both go. I won't tell anyone about you."

"That is true," Vee said sadly. "You will not tell. You will not be able to."

"Why?" Terror twisted in my gut.

"You should not have followed me. I only have until noon tomorrow to complete my mission and you are an unfortunate complication."

"I— I promise to keep your secret."

"It is no use, Cassie. I have to follow rules or suffer grave punishments when I return home. I am so, so sorry. Goodbye, friend."

Vee reached behind her back, then brought her arms forward and aimed a large black metal gun directly at me.

chapter sixteen

Holding On To
the Memories

"WAIT! Don't shoot!" My mind raced for some sort of delay. I couldn't believe this was really happening. I was in a spaceship, talking to an alien, and facing the barrel of a very dangerous-looking gun. Yikes! Think fast, Cassie!

"Why not?" Vee asked impatiently. "This will not hurt, I promise."

"Easy for you to say! You're the one pointing the gun!"

"Gun?" She shook Amber's blond curls. "This is not a gun. It's a *babbzonk*."

This was too much for my tiny human brain to take in. Maybe I should have been born a mosquito with a big, ruby-red doodlezapp.

"Okay, I give. What's a babbzonk?"

"A harmless tool to make you forget. A small zonk will erase the past few days. A medium zonk and you'll forget several weeks. You don't even want to know what a large zonk will do." She smiled sadly. "I am only going to give you a small zonk—just enough to forget my rebotco and me."

She aimed the babbzonk again . . .

"NO! WAIT!" I cried desperately. "There has to be a better way. Tell me about your mission. Maybe I can help you."

"Doubtful," Vee said skeptically. "You have no special powers to find my *zillofax*. You are only human."

"Humans are good at finding things. Uh, what's a zillofax?"

"An object of utmost importance. I have to get it back before I leave Earth tomorrow or I will be in big trouble."

"How big is it? What does it look like?" I asked.

"It is the size of the slim, black box your father carries."

"His briefcase?" I guessed.

Vee nodded. "Except my zillofax is the color of this doodlezapp." Still aiming her weapon at me, she reached into the basket and drew out a gleaming, golden-yellow marble.

"Gold? A zillofax is gold?"

"In color. While I was flying over the campground a week ago, it fell out of my rebotco. But I have searched through the campground and cannot find it." Vee's lip trembled the way Amber's did when she was about to cry.

"It'll be all right." My gaze zeroed in on the wicked-looking babbzonk. I wondered if I could knock it out of her hands, figure out how to open the door, and then escape . . .

"Nothing will be all right if I do not find my zillofax. Severe punishment, and my rebotco will be taken away. I'll be grounded on my own boring planet!" Vee sounded desperate.

"Grounded? I've been grounded too, and it stinks."

"I have looked and looked, but my zillofax is gone. Still I must keep searching." She straightened her shoulders and steadied her babbzonk. "Talking wastes time. Once your memory is altered, we will return to camp together. No one will know I am not the real Amber. Not even you."

"WAIT!"

"No more waiting."

"But I can help you find your zill-o-whatever." I put my hands in front of my face protectively. I could tell by her determined gaze that my protests were useless. She was going to take away my memory—which sounded as scary as being riddled with bullets. And what about Amber? How could I rescue her if I couldn't even remember she was missing?

Remember . . . remember . . .

Something clicked in my head.

"*Vee!* Don't mess with my memory! Not if you want to find your zillofax."

"Why? Do you know where my zillofax is? Or are you still stalling? I do not have time for games."

"No game. Honest!" I hopped in place because it would be harder for Vee to hit a moving target. "I just remembered something important."

"What?"

"I know who has your zillofax."

chapter seventeen

A Promise

"**W**ho?" Vee sounded like she wanted to trust me but was afraid.

Of course, I was afraid to trust her, too. If I told her what I suspected, she could still babbzonk me.

"I need to show you."

"This had better not be a trick."

"It's for real. If everything works out, you'll have your zillofax back soon." I arched my eyebrows, challenging her. "But on one condition."

"Yes?"

"You get your zillofax and I get Amber."

"Once I have my zillofax, I have no need for Amber. It is a promise."

"*A promise*," I echoed.

And when she lowered her babbzonk, I let out a sigh of relief. My memory was safe and so was I . . . for now.

chapter eighteen

Bad News
Gets Worse

"Mom! Dad! We're back!" I exclaimed as I hurried toward my camp with Vee following behind me.

It felt so good to see my mother sitting at the table wearing a crown made of pine needles and Lucas stabbing shadows with his stick-sword. My family. I never wanted to leave them again. I only wished Amber were here.

Then I noticed the black Chevy parked beside our van.

I recognized the bumper sticker, which read "Behind every successful woman is a man who is surprised." But why had Monica Dumano, the producer for *I Don't Believe It!*, driven up here?

Glancing around, I didn't see Ms. Dumano or my father, only Mom, Lucas, and Dribble.

Vee came up beside me. "Why is there another car at the campsite?" she whispered.

"I'm not sure. It belongs to the producer for Dad's show, Ms. Dumano. I bet it has something to do with Mr. Lester."

"The man with the mean dogs?"

"Very vicious dogs." I shuddered, remembering clinging to the branch and feeling doggie breath on my ankle. But then I smiled because I was so glad to still have that memory. "And Mr. Lester is even meaner than his dogs."

"Is Mr. Lester the one?" Vee lowered her voice as we stepped into the campsite.

"I think so. He told Dad he found a gold thingamajig, which sounds like your zillofax." I nodded toward Monica Dumano's car. "I'll know more once I find out why Ms. Dumano is here. Go play with your duck while I talk to Mom."

Vee glanced with disgust at the mud hole where Dribble was splashing. "No. I'll stay close to you."

Mom put down the *Homespun Harvest* magazine she'd been reading when she noticed us. "Where have you girls been?" she demanded. "It doesn't take an hour to visit the outhouse or dump the garbage. I was getting worried."

"No reason to worry," Vee said sweetly.

"I know, honey. But moms are expert worriers. Cassie should have known better to stay away so long—especially when she has chores to do."

I clenched my jaw. It wasn't fair how Mom always blamed me. Even when Amber wasn't Amber, she got away with everything.

"We didn't mean to take so long," I explained. "We found a hiking path and lost track of time."

"Next time tell me before you go exploring." Mom sipped her iced herbal tea. "Was your hike fun?"

"Fun? Yeah . . . sorta," I said with an uncertain glance at Vee. "I saw amazing things."

"I hoped you kids would learn to respect nature this weekend." Mom stared off in a dreamy way. "My own childhood camping memories are very dear to me."

"Memories are important," I said. "I don't want to ever forget anything."

"Don't count on that, Cass." Vee winked at me.

I didn't like her wink. I was glad we were becoming friends, but I couldn't trust her. I would sure be glad when Amber was Amber again. Wearily, I sank down on the bench beside my mother.

Mom put her arm around me. "Your father and I want you kids to have special memories, too, like picnics, visiting the zoo, trips to the beach, and now this campout. I'm so glad this outdoor experience is a success."

"But is it a success for Dad?" I asked pointedly. "Is that why he isn't here and Ms. Dumano's car is? Are they talking to Mr. Lester right now?"

"Cassie! *Shssh!*" She put her finger to her lips. "Your father's work is not your concern."

"But I am concerned. Are Dad and Ms. Dumano at Mr. Lester's campsite?" I persisted. "Did Ms. Dumano bring a cameraman? Are they filming right now?"

"I hope so," Mom said as she ran her fingers through her curly hair. "Your father is planning to expose Mr. Lester's scam. I can't go into details, but Mr. Lester has a history of fraud. His UFO sighting is a hoax."

"But his picture looked real," I said.

"Pictures are easily faked. The idea of a flying saucer here is ridiculous!"

"Ridiculous," I said with a forced smile.

Vee chuckled. "Everyone knows spaceships and aliens are not real."

I gave her a stern glance warning her not to make Mom suspicious. It was bad enough Dribble continued to avoid "Amber." And I'd noticed Lucas watching Vee-Amber curiously.

"Amber, let's go take another walk." I tugged on her hand.

"Okay."

"Hold it right there, girls," Mom said, putting her hands up like an officer stopping traffic. "You've done too much walking and not enough working. Cassie, there are still dishes to wash. Amber, it isn't fair for Lucas to babysit your duck. Dribble is your responsibility."

I frowned at the pile of dirty dishes.

Vee frowned at Dribble.

"But Mom," I whined, "we're here in the outdoors to enjoy nature. Amber and I want to collect more pinecones so we can decorate them."

"Or eat them," Vee put in eagerly.

I squeezed her fingers hard and shot her a nasty look. Then I turned back to Mom with my nicest smile. "Come on, Mom, I'll wash later. It's too nice of a day to stay at camp."

"Well . . ." I knew Mom was wavering. She was probably visualizing the pinecone decorations.

Before she could say anything else, there were footsteps and loud voices. I looked up the dirt road and saw three figures heading our way: Dad, Ms. Dumano, and a cameraman named Fred. Dad did not look happy.

"That's it!" Dad shouted as he stormed into camp. "We're out of here! Pack up the tents, clear the campsite, and we're gone, pronto!"

"Jon?" Mom questioned, immediately coming over to lay her hand on Dad's arm. "What is it? What happened?"

"That . . . that CROOK!" Dad's eyes burned with fury.

"Mr. Lester?" I guessed.

"Of course, Mr. Lester. Who else?" Dad slapped his briefcase on the picnic table. "I suspected he was only after the million dollars, and now I know it. Only that isn't even enough for him. He demanded two million just to look at his alien find."

"That's absurd," Ms. Dumano said with a flip of her black hair. She was younger than my parents, yet worried so much she had deep lines in her fore-head. If every detail of the TV show wasn't perfect, she stressed out completely. And she was so fashion conscious, she always wore sleek black slacks or skirts and designer blouses with fitted jackets—even on a campout.

"We should consult our lawyers." Ms. Dumano sighed. "I wonder what Mr. Lester found."

"Well . . . most likely, maybe, it's probably a fake," Cameraman Fred said in a drawl as he rubbed his stubby gray-brown beard. His relaxed, ex-hippie attitude was a contrast to uptight Ms. Dumano. It took him forever to make a decision, but he was quick when it came to filming the perfect shot.

"Of course it's a fake." Dad frowned. "What else could it be?"

"A chance to hit top ratings for *I Don't Believe It!*" Monica shot Dad a hopeful look.

But Dad just shook his head. "Nothing is worth dealing with a loser like Lester. I'm ready to pack up now."

"No!" I cried, grabbing Dad's arm. "We have to stay."

"Cassie, this is not your business." Dad gave me a sizzling look. "And it's not mine anymore either. Hey, I gave it a shot. Came up here on a wild space-ship chase, but it didn't work out."

Ms. Dumano flipped her hair back again. "But that's exactly the kind of show we do best. Come on, Jon."

"No show," Dad said firmly. "Didn't you hear Lester threaten to set his dogs on us? He wasn't kidding either. He's dangerous."

I gulped. Dad was right about that.

"Simmer down, Jon, simmer down. Let's decide in the morning," Cameraman-Fred said in his slow drawl.

"I brought a tent," Monica added.

Dad grumbled some more, but eventually he calmed down and agreed to stay another night. Only he was firm—he would not make a deal with Mr. Lester.

Which meant Mr. Lester would not return Vee's gold zillofax.

"Darn that greedy Mr. Lester," I told Vee when we were alone in our tent. "I don't know how we'll get your zillofax from him. I'm really sorry."

"You will be sorry if my zillofax isn't returned," she replied with a dangerous gleam in her fake violet eyes.

"But it's not my fault! I can't make Mr. Lester give it to us!"

"You have to figure out a way or—"

"Or what?" I dug my fingers into my sleeping bag.

"My ship is automatically set to leave tomorrow by noon. I can't change that without my zillofax. And since Amber is already on my rebotco, she will have to return with me. For her lifetime."

chapter nineteen

Hopeless
and Helpless

"Dad! You have to pay the two million!" I raced out of the tent and rushed to my father. "You'd pay millions for a ransom if one of us kids was kidnapped, wouldn't you?"

"I'd give my life for my family," Dad said. "But Mr. Lester hasn't kidnapped anyone. He's a two-bit swindler trying to make some easy cash with a phony story and ridiculous threats."

"But if one of us kids—" I paused to gulp a deep breath, glancing at Vee who had come up beside me. "Let's say, just for example, that Amber was held for ransom—you'd pay two million, right?"

"For Amber?" Dad ripped open a bag of baby carrots and grinned. "Two million is kind of steep. Maybe one million."

"Dad this is *not* a joke. It's important. Amber's life depends on it."

"Is that so?" Dad jokingly tugged on one of Vee's curls. "Amber, is your life in danger? Funny, but you look fine to me. What game are you kids playing?"

"Not a game." Vee jerked away from Dad and smoothed her hair in place. "I want the zil . . . gold object."

"I want it, too—to prove it's a fake. But I will not pay for news."

"Dad, you don't understand!" I cried. "Amber, do something so he'll believe us. Blow pink bubbles with your najlem, show your spaceship, or speak in an alien language."

"What?" Vee blinked innocently. "I don't know what you're talking about, Cassie." She sounded exactly like Amber.

The grownups were all giving me "what a cute imagination" looks—the same looks usually reserved for Lucas when he is portraying a character. Even Lucas was chuckling.

No one believed me.

Clenching my fists at my sides, I fought feelings of hurt, anger, and fear. If Dad wouldn't pay the ransom, Mr. Lester might find someone else to buy his gold thingamajig, then Vee would zoom into space with my sister.

And there was nothing I could do. I had no alien powers. Of course, I had told Vee that humans were good at trying. So, that's what I'd do. Try very, very, *very* hard.

But how in the world was I going to convince Mr. Lester to give me his two-million-dollar treasure?

chapter twenty

Inside the Enemy's Camp

The sun had begun a slow descent in the west, sinking sleepily behind a mountain, cooling the campsite with long shadows. The chilly air felt refreshing, but less sun meant more mosquitoes, and those pesky bloodsuckers kept buzzing around me. Maybe their doodlezapps were big, but a swat of my hand and squirt of bugspray proved me the superior being.

"When are we going after my zillofax?" Vee whispered. We sat at the picnic table and glued sparkly red, white, and blue sequins on pinecones. Nearby, Lucas used a flashlight to read a comic book with a white knight on the cover, while Dribble rested peacefully on his lap.

"Wait until it's safe to sneak away," I said, with an uneasy glance at the grownups. Mom, Dad, Ms. Dumano, and Fred were chatting over a game of dominos on a card table.

"I want to go now." Vee sounded exactly like Amber in one of her spoiled brat moods.

"Soon." I reached for a jar of red glitter and sprinkled some over my pinecone. "But we don't want anyone to get suspicious, so act like you're having fun."

"I am having fun." Vee glued a blue bead on her pinecone. "These tree snacks will taste good with sparkles."

"Those sparkles are called glitter," I explained. "And you don't eat them."

"Then what is their purpose?"

"To look pretty."

Vee scrunched her nose, as if this puzzled her. Then she stared at her decorated pinecone and gave a slow nod. "I think I understand. Working on this cone is an accomplishment."

"Yeah. I just wish I could accomplish something really important. Prove to everyone I'm more than the oldest child," I added with a sigh. Then I closed the lid on the glitter. "Mom just went in her tent. Let's sneak out to Mr. Lester's now."

"I don't want to go there."

"Why not?"

"I do not like dogs." Vee glanced down, as if embarrassed. "I'm not like the real Amber. I only brought animals on this trip because my galactic species instructor insisted. I don't like animals from any planet. Not even cuddly goofinks."

"What are they?"

"Tiny, big-eyed, furry pets that love to curl around arms or wrists. They make a soft, cooing sound and are very playful. But I avoid them. Even Dribble scares me."

"A little duck scares you? But that's crazy! You shouldn't be afraid of anything. You have your babbzonk to protect you."

"My babbzonk does not work on animals. It is not a weapon; it simply alters memory. I have no real weapons. I'm not old enough to carry a *doowta* yet."

"What about that pink bubble potato?"

"My najlem is a sonic bubble tool for contacting my rebotco ship. It is only a remote control device."

"You mean, you have no special powers? Like a *human*?"

"I can't fly or turn invisible if that is what you mean. And animals make me nervous."

I almost laughed. I had been afraid of Vee, yet she had more fears than I did. Imagine being afraid of a duck!

But I had to give Vee credit; even though she was scared, she agreed to go to the Lester camp. I told my parents that "Amber" and I were going to the outhouse. We took a flashlight, since it was almost dark, and then left camp.

Fifteen minutes later (after a quick stop at the outhouse), Vee and I huddled in the bushes outside Mr. Lester's trailer. Except for a small lantern on an outside table, the campsite was dark and silent. Eerily silent.

"Let's go back. No one is here," Vee said.

"Not so fast." I pulled her forward. "This is a lucky break! Since no one's here, we can search for your zillofax."

"But I do not want to meet those dogs."

"I'm not eager to run into them either. I love animals, but Brutus and Julius are just plain mean."

"Where . . . where are they?"

"Maybe Mr. Lester took them for a walk. Their doghouses look empty." I gestured to two large crates at the side of the trailer. There were bars and locks on each crate—top-notch, secure doggie prisons.

"I bet the zillofax is in the trailer." I stepped around the campfire pit and stared at the shabby white trailer.

Swallowing my fear, I reached out to twist the knob. I expected it to be locked, but it wasn't. The door easily swung open.

"Are we going in there?" Vee asked.

"If you want to find your zillofax, we have to."

Vee gulped. The door clanged shut behind us. I shone my flashlight around the narrow, cramped trailer and used my free hand to pinch my nose. Boy, did this place stink! Dirty dishes were piled in the sink, empty beer cans on the tiny counter, a Sugar Sweetems cereal box, bags of chips, rumpled piles of clothes, and dark stains on the floor. Were the stains blood from Mr. Lester's latest victims? Or did the dog-beasts need to be potty trained?

Vee was peeking in cupboards and corners. So I searched, too, but I only found smelly socks and positive proof that the dogs flunked their potty-training lessons.

I started to leave the kitchen when I spotted a notepad by a cell phone. A name I recognized too well was scrawled by a phone number: Sebastian Mooncroft—also known as Mystical Mooncroft!

"What's wrong?" Vee asked, coming up beside me.

I showed her the notepad. "Look!"

"So?" She shrugged.

"Mr. Lester may plan to sell the zillofax to another TV show. Although I don't think *Mooncroft's Miracles* can afford two million dollars. Any sign of the zillofax?"

"No. It is not here," Vee said with disappointment. "Where else do we look?"

"How about the truck?"

Vee and I hurried outside, but the truck was locked. Obviously, Mr. Lester valued it more than he did his trailer. The windows were surprisingly clean, and when we shone the flashlight through them, there was no sign of the zillofax—only discarded fast-food containers.

We'd been in the campsite for over fifteen minutes. We had to leave soon. But there were still two places to search: the doghouses.

My hand trembled as I aimed the flashlights at the dark, forbidding cages. The perfect hiding place for something valuable—especially when the beasts were imprisoned inside.

"No," Vee said, backing away. "I cannot crawl in there."

"Someone has to check it out."

"I will hold the flashlight for you," Vee offered.

"Thanks," I said sarcastically. "You're *soooo* considerate."

"Anytime." She smiled nervously, then snatched the flashlight from my hands.

I took a deep breath and knelt down on the ground. A rock dug into one of my knees, I winced, then shifted my leg. It's just a doghouse, I told myself.

The first doghouse was totally empty, except for kibble crumbs, a blanket, and an empty water dish.

But the second dog house had ripped rags, torn papers, sticks, chewed Frisbees, and a lumpy blanket in the far back.

"There's something yellow under the blanket!" I exclaimed.

"My zillofax!" Vee rejoiced, bending over to give me more light.

"I can't tell. It's too far back for the light to reach. I'll have to feel for it." I shivered, hoping I didn't touch creepy bugs or dog poop. "I'm reaching . . . I've got the blanket . . . I'm pulling it off . . . but it's not gold . . . it's . . . it's . . ."

I screamed.

chapter twenty-one

Pet Poochie
Panic

"Bones! Long, large bones!" I cried, backing out of the doghouse at warp speed. "Mr. Lester is a *murderer!*"

I turned and ran. I'd known Mr. Lester was a creep, but I didn't know he was a *murderer*. And feeding his poor, innocent victims to those dog-demons! Despicable!

"Slow down, Cassie," Vee cried, chasing after me.

"Can't! Gotta tell Dad." I broke through bushes and sped down the dirt road. Dad would know what to do. In fact, this could turn out to be great for his TV show: *I Don't Believe It!* uncovers a murderer and his monster dogs.

"No, Cassie! Stop!" Vee grabbed my arm to slow me down. "Think for a minute! Those bones cannot be human."

"Why not?" I stopped to stare at her.

"Big dogs chew big bones. But not people bones. And there was no skull."

"You're right." My heart slowed a little. "I guess I let my imagination get away with me. Mr. Lester probably wouldn't kill anyone . . . I think."

"That's right." Vee stepped over a deep rut in the dirt road. "Besides, you cannot tell your parents about me or my zillofax."

"Don't worry." I leaned against my knees to catch my breath. "I— I didn't plan to."

"That's wise."

"No one would believe me anyway." I straightened up and faced my sister-substitute. "I'd just get in trouble for sneaking off to Mr. Lester's campsite."

"The parents would be very angry. And they would interfere with our search. Where else can we look for my zillofax?"

"Nowhere tonight. It's too dark."

Neither of us spoke as we walked back to camp. There was nothing left to say. I had failed. It was hopeless. Maybe Amber would enjoy living on another planet.

I tried to cheer myself up by thinking of good things. It was good that Mr. Lester's trailer had been unlocked. We didn't know where the zillofax was, but we did know where it wasn't. And we'd been lucky Mr. Lester hadn't caught us snooping. That was one nasty dude I didn't want to see again.

Never. Ever. Again.

So when Vee and I stepped into our campsite, I nearly fell over.

Mr. Lester and his vicious pets were there!

chapter twenty-two
No Deal!

The dogs offered their usual welcome: drooling fangs, guttural growls, and demonic stares. The devil beasts lunged on their leashes, hungry for a quick kiddie snack.

I reached out protectively toward Vee. She dug her fingernails into my skin. To say she was scared was an understatement. Pull out a thesaurus and you'll find more fitting words: Aghast, anxious, appalled, horrified, petrified, shocked, spooked, and paralyzed with pulsating terror.

"Down, Brutus!" Mr. Lester ordered, with a snort of annoyance. "Cut it out, Julius! You already had your eats, so shut your stupid, good-for-nothing traps." The dogs instantly silenced. Sit, heel, they obeyed. They even hung their heads, as if shamed before their master.

Mom shot the dogs and their owner a nasty look, then jumped out of her lawn chair and put her arms around "Amber" and me. "You girls all right?"

"Yes, Mom," we both replied.

Lucas came over and asked suspiciously, "Where were you?"

"Walking," I said with a shrug.

"Where? You've both been acting sneaky. What's going on?"

"Nothing."

"I don't buy that. You've got a secret. Tell me the truth."

"You couldn't handle it," I joked.

Lucas stared at us with a thoughtful, curious expression that made me uneasy. He probably would have asked more questions, only Mr. Lester called Dad a word that caught our attentions.

"Mr. Lester!" Mom exclaimed. "Don't use that language in front of my children!"

"I'll say whatever I dang well please." Mr. Lester glared at my father. "You heard my final offer, Strange."

"And you heard my final reply, Lester." Dad lifted his head high. "If your find proves to be authentic, you will receive the million dollars. But not two million and certainly not without first seeing what you have."

"You're making a big mistake." Mr. Lester spat on the ground and jerked on the leashes. "I'll take my gold thingamajig to another show."

"Be my guest. But you'll find no one will pay without proof."

"We'll see about that! I already called a pack of media types and they'll be at my camp for an important press conference at one tomorrow. Someone will fork over big bucks and you'll be sorry."

"I wish you luck," Dad said politely, yet there was a sharp edge to his voice.

"I'll drop my price to one million. It's a great deal for a real alien object."

"No deal," Dad said firmly.

"Have it your way!" he growled. "Your reputation will stink like a sewer when I tell everyone how you passed up this chance. No one will believe you or your show again."

"Our business is over," Dad said with narrowed eyes. "Leave now before I do something I regret."

"Fine! And don't come sniffing around my camp after my gold thingamajig. 'Cause it's hid somewhere no one can find."

"I believe my husband asked you to leave," my mother put in coolly. "And don't come back."

"I won't, you can be sure of that!" He snapped the leashes and strode off with his bone-chewing beasts.

Beside me, Vee frowned and wrung her hands together. I was worried, too, but I felt something else: pride for my parents. They were so cool.

"Good riddance to bad rubbish," Ms. Dumano said, flipping back her thick hair and snapping open a small makeup compact for a quick touch-up.

"Hey, all right, let's celebrate." Fred pulled out a harmonica. "Anyone up for some campfire songs? Bet you didn't know I was an Eagle Scout. I can start a fire without kindling and blow out some nifty tunes on my harmonica."

"Sounds great!" Dad said with enthusiasm.

"I'll get some organic marshmallows for roasting," Mom suggested.

"Splendid!" Ms. Dumano exclaimed. "And I know a shivery story perfect for a dark night in the mountains. Have any of you heard of the river witch ghost?"

We shook our heads. Then Ms. Dumano launched into a scary tale.

Songs around a campfire. Roasted marshmallows. And even spooky storytelling. I couldn't believe it! At last, the Strange family was doing normal camping stuff. My dream was finally coming true.

Almost.

If only Amber were here . . .

chapter twenty-three
Trick or Terror

I woke up the next morning with a Plan.

If my plan were fireworks, it would light up the sky like the Fourth of July. When I told Vee, she nearly jumped out of her fake skin with excitement.

"Excellent idea. Let's do it now!" Vee slipped off Amber's nightgown and changed into cutoffs and a T-shirt.

"I'm not even dressed."

"So get dressed." Vee glanced through the tent opening at the sky, as if consulting a clock. "It is almost seven. That gives us five hours."

"I better leave a note saying we're on a walk. Also, we should eat breakfast," I said as I tied my shoelaces.

"Snack on a pinecone."

"Pinecone?" I stuck out my tongue. "No, thanks. Maybe a banana. And you can eat the peel."

"Yummy." Vee tugged on my arm, pulling me out of the tent. "I love banana peels even more than pinecones."

I shook my head. Aliens sure had weird appetites.

• • •

Minutes later, Vee and I were ready to leave camp. Almost ready, anyway. First we needed a few important tools for our plan: a boom box, a loud rap CD, and a talented actor.

Lucas was startled when I asked if I could "hire" him for an acting job. I found a dollar in my pocket and offered it to him.

"My first paying job!" He snatched the money, then regarded me suspiciously. "But what's this all about? I knew you and Amber were up to something. What?"

"I'll explain after you help us." I looked at Vee nervously. "I will be able to remember, won't I?"

Vee smiled sweetly. "If I get you-know-what."

"So that's it!" Lucas snapped his fingers. "Now I understand."

"You do?" Vee and I exclaimed at the same time.

"Sure." He leaned close for a conspiratorial wink. "You want me to create a diversion so you can smuggle a pet into camp. What is it this time? A rabbit, a raccoon—or a baby cougar?"

"A zillofax," Vee said.

"Whatever." He rolled his eyes. "So don't tell me."

"This is about more than pets. We're trying to help Dad," I added honestly. "I'm worried Mr. Lester could ruin Dad's reputation."

"No one threatens my dad and gets away with it." Lucas picked up his stick sword and waved it. "I'll challenge Lester to a duel and skewer the errant knave."

"No skewering needed. Only acting." How can my brother have such a high IQ and still be so clueless?

"Acting is in my blood," he said with a swish of his sword. "You can count on me to give a convincing performance."

But we couldn't count on Dribble to keep quiet, so we left the duck in our tent with some lettuce and water. I'd have a soggy mess to clean up later.

Vee, Lucas, and I headed for Mr. Lester's camp.

As we neared the camp, I gave the signal for Vee to turn on the boom box. "Now, Vee. Blast away with the music. And make it loud."

"Very loud," Lucas added, wrapping his cloak around his shoulders in spy-fashion. "Our suspect will be under surveillance soon. Or my name isn't Strange. Lucas Strange."

Lucas had switched from shining knight to James Bond, I realized with a groan.

Vee switched on the boom box. We stood on the road just outside Mr. Lester's trailer. When rap music blared, Brutus and Julius sprang to life with ferocious barking. The junky trailer swayed. A deep, cranky voice swore—words I wouldn't dare repeat.

"The prime suspect has been awakened." Lucas held a rock to his mouth as if it were a walkie-talkie. "Stand by while I give an Oscar-worthy performance. Over and out."

"Put away the rock, 007." I turned to Vee. "Ready, Amber?"

"Yes." Vee's gaze was on the growling dogs as she nodded.

As soon as Mr. Lester poked his head out of his trailer, we started talking loud enough for him to hear.

"Isn't it great that Dad is going to get the gold thingamajig after all?" Lucas began dramatically.

I hoped Mr. Lester would take the bait and think we were enjoying an innocent morning walk. It was natural that we'd discuss our father. And a lowlife like Mr. Lester couldn't resist eavesdropping.

The trailer door opened wider . . .

"It's SO cool that someone found the gold thing and is giving it to Dad for free," I fibbed.

"Really cool," Vee added.

Out of the corner of my eye, I saw Mr. Lester's startled expression. He shushed his dogs and crept closer. It was hard not to laugh, though, because he was wearing white boxer shorts with red kissy lips dotted all over them.

"Dad is SO excited," Lucas went on.

"Very excited," I echoed.

Vee grinned. "Now he will learn that aliens are real."

I poked her in the side, and shot a warning look. "Stop kidding, Amber. You know aliens aren't real. Dad will prove it."

"In front of thousands, maybe millions, of viewers," Lucas added. "Our family will be famous! Paparazzi will surround us and snap our pictures, even steal our garbage. We'll be mobbed by autograph seekers. Casting agents will offer me movie roles—"

"Enough already!" I shushed my over-acting brother. "We have to go back to camp now."

"Returning to camp!" Lucas announced.

"We're leaving," Vee announced.

I rolled my eyes. Of course, we only pretended to leave.

We walked down the road, ducked behind bushes and laughed over Mr. Lester's kissy-lips shorts. Then we grew serious. I convinced Lucas to go back to our campsite by saying it was his duty to guard our family.

"Real spy stuff," I told him. And he fell for it.

Vee and I circled back, then cut through dense brush and huddled behind thick bushes.

"Will I get my zillofax soon?" Vee asked.

"I hope so. Mr. Lester heard what we said, so he'll go off to check his hiding place—which will lead us to your zillofax." I grabbed Vee's hand. "Look! He's leaving!"

Staying a safe distance behind Mr. Lester, Vee and I began to follow.

"He's taking those beasts!" Vee complained.

"Be extra quiet so they don't hear us."

"What if they smell us?" she asked, fearfully.

"Dogs have amazing smelling abilities. I know all

about Earth animals from my galactic species class."

"We won't get too close," I assured. "We can watch from a safe distance."

We stopped talking when Mr. Lester left the main road and took a narrow deer trail. We climbed uphill and my breath came out in quick gasps. After hopping over a narrow ravine, we climbed up an even steeper path. A wall of mountain loomed before us, and my heart lurched.

How far and high would we have to go?

"You okay?" I whispered to Vee, as I leaned against a mossy bolder. Mr. Lester had paused up ahead to shake a pebble from his boot.

"Yeah." Her skin seemed unusually shiny. "But it's after nine already. My spaceship is set to leave at noon—whether I'm on it or not."

"*No!*" I cried softly. And in my anxious heart, my sister's name echoed. *Oh, Amber!*

But I wasn't able to ask any more questions, because Mr. Lester was on the move again. Around trees, over granite boulders, across dry creek beds, and through high, scratchy weeds. Just when I thought my lungs would burst from exhaustion, the dogs suddenly stopped by a rotting, fallen pine tree.

"The dogs are sniffing the ground," I whispered, pointing.

"One of the beasts is digging!" Vee's voice rose hopefully. "This is it, Cassie. It must be my zillofax! At last!"

"*Shhsh*!" I cautioned.

But it was too late.

"What was that?" Mr. Lester barked. "Who's there? Show yourself or I'll let my dogs find ya for me."

The dogs jerked on their leashes, snarled, growled, and aimed their demonic fangs directly toward the bushes where Vee and I were hiding.

chapter twenty-four
Zonked

Vee and I clung to each other. The fact that a small piece of her skin flaked off of her hand didn't bother me.

"Come out now or here go the dogs," Mr. Lester threatened, and I knew he meant it.

Slowly, I stood to surrender.

Vee moved beside me.

Brutus and Julius jerked on their leashes, but Mr. Lester snapped them back. "You're Strange's daughters." He seemed genuinely surprised. "What are you kids doing out here?"

Vee looked too scared to speak, so I answered, "We were . . . uh . . . hiking."

"This far from camp?" He squinted at us. "I'm not fallin' for that hogwash. You were tracking me, and I know why. You're after my alien discovery."

"No, no . . . that's not it," I lied.

"You can't trick me, girlie."

"I don't know what you're talking about."

"Tell me the truth!" he barked. "Or deal with my dogs."

Vee stared at Mr. Lester like he was the alien and she was a helpless human. She scooted closer to me, as if I could protect her. Me? Protect someone else?

But someone had to stand up to Mr. Lester, and Vee wasn't volunteering.

"Really, we were just hiking," I insisted. "We saw you walking your dogs and came over to say hi . . . uh . . . Hi."

"Don't lie, girlie. Did your father put you up to this?"

"No. He told us to stay away from you."

"You should have listened to your daddy." He took a menacing step toward us. "My alien thinga-majig is safe in a hidden place and no one is going to stop me from selling it for big bucks."

"Just let us go." My eyes focused not on Mr. Lester, but on his trained attack animals. If the chains were released, I was sure that Vee's and my bones would join the others in that doghouse.

"I can't let you go yakking to your dad. I got no aim to hurt little girls, but I can order my dogs to guard you out here so you don't interfere with my press conference."

"Vee!" I cried. "Do something!"

"I-I can't . . ."

"Begging your baby sister for help? Oh, how brave!" Mr. Lester's gruff chuckle mocked me. "What's the pretty little girlie gonna do? Frown? Pout? Throw a tantrum?"

"She's not a little girl!" I yelled. "Come on, Vee. Snap out of it. Use your space weapons!"

She shook her head. "I told you I don't have real weapons."

"Weapons? Going to tie me up with a pretty hair ribbon?" He laughed even louder. "Throw a dolly at me?"

"Vee!" I pleaded. "Please!"

Mr. Lester laughed even harder.

"Well . . . there is something." Vee reached into her pocket. A tense, desperate expression crossed her face, and then she sprung her arms forward . . . now holding her babbzonk.

"What's that toy?" Mr. Lester asked, coming closer. "Does it squirt water or—"

ZOOOOOOOONK!

Vee's hands exploded with a burst of noise and a swirling tornado that swallowed Mr. Lester whole; churning dust, kicking up rocks and leaves, and sounding like a thunderous tidal wave.

The dogs yelped as they were knocked off their paws. Entangled in their own chains, they lay stunned on the ground.

I heard a terrified cry from Mr. Lester, but I couldn't see through the babbzonk tornado. This was not a small, medium, or even large zonk. Vee had let him have a *humongous* zonk.

When the dust settled, the noise died down, and the world stood still, I stared in shock at Mr. Lester.

chapter twenty-five

Baby and the Beasts

Mr. Lester had changed.

Oh, he looked the same—black beard, scruffy clothes, worn leather boots—but he was clearly different. He sat on the ground with his thumb in his mouth and drool dribbling down his chin. And what was that dark stain on his pants?

"Baa, gaa, baa," Mr. Lester cooed.

"Vee!" I cried. "What's happened to him?"

"His memory has been altered."

"*How* altered?"

"Back to his diaper days." She grinned mischievously, the babbzonk shrinking to the size of a comb, then disappearing into her pocket. "Do diapers come in adult super-duper large?"

"Diapers? You mean!" My hands flew to my face in astonishment. "Mr. Lester is . . . is a baby! Impossible!"

"Aliens aren't real either." Vee chuckled, then went over and patted Mr. Lester on the head. "Nice baby boy."

I still was trying to deal with the fact that a grown man had been transformed into a gurgling baby. Mr. Lester couldn't even walk! And now he was playing with his fingers. He couldn't hurt us anymore, but he couldn't help us either.

"Vee! This is terrible." I watched Mr. Lester scoop up dirt and put it in his mouth.

"Why? Mr. Lester is not harmed. When he returns to normal in an hour, he will remember nothing."

"But we don't have an hour," I pointed out. "How will we find the zillofax without him?"

"Oh . . . I did not think of that." Vee's face crumpled. "I've ruined everything!"

"You didn't have a choice. Mr. Lester was threatening us."

"But now I will have to leave without my zillofax," cried Vee.

"Would that really be so terrible? I've been wondering . . ." I walked over to her, careful to avoid the dogs who were still stunned and entangled in their leashes. "Why do you want the zillofax so badly?"

"It's important to my studies and it contains codes to help me run my rebotco. It represents months of research. But it's gone now." Her lower lip trembled.

"We can still look for it. The dogs led us to this spot, so the zillofax must be nearby."

"Good point." Vee perked up, then walked over to a half-dug area of dirt. "See the paw marks. They were digging here."

"So we will, too," I said.

I found a stick and began to dig. As I worked, I glanced at my watch. It was nearly eleven! Only one hour before the rebotco would take off with Amber aboard.

"I found something!" Vee cried out. She bent over her hole and shoveled dirt away with her hands. "It's solid . . . It has to be my zillofax."

Kneeling beside her, I helped dig. I could feel something solid, too. Smooth, yellow . . . oh, no!

Not again!

"Another dog bone!" Vee cried.

"That's why the dogs were digging," I added, feeling as if my last hope had been buried in the ground with that bone.

"My zillofax is gone forever," Vee sobbed.

"I'm sorry, so very sorry." My voice cracked. "But it isn't Amber's fault. Please let her go."

"There's not enough time to reprogram the ship." Vee shook her blond curls. "But don't worry, Amber will like my planet. And I always wanted a sister."

"But you can't take *my* sister." A wild thought jumped into my head. "Take me instead."

"You?" Vee's fake violet-blue eyes widened. "I hadn't thought of that."

"Think fast, Vee. There isn't much time."

"Fifty-two minutes."

"Take me, Vee. My family won't miss me as much as Amber."

"Why not?" she asked softly.

"I don't have any special talent." I swallowed hard, aware that my words could change my life forever. "Lucas can act, Amber understands animals, my Dad has a TV show, and Mom fights to save the environment. I don't do anything important on Earth so I might as well go to another planet."

"That's not true."

"If you have to take a human, I'm your Earthling." I held out my arms, surrendering, pretending to be brave. Goodbye trees, goodbye dirt, goodbye world.

"But I think you have a special talent."

"A talent for getting into trouble?"

"Perhaps," Vee said with a chuckle. "But also a talent for seeking the truth. For trying hard even when things seem impossible. Many humans believe what others tell them without thinking for themselves. Your parents told you aliens weren't real. But you searched for your own truth . . . and you found me."

A talent for seeing the truth? Could Vee be right?

"Will you take me instead of Amber?" I asked hopefully.

"I wish I could, but there is no time for a switch. Amber has already been prepared for space travel," she answered sadly. "I must contact my ship and leave before it's too late."

"NO!" I grabbed her hand. "There's still forty-three minutes. We can find your zillofax."

"Not without Mr. Lester's help. No one else knows the hidden location."

"Are you sure about that?" A wild, desperate, truly wacko idea jumped in my head. "Mr. Lester isn't the only one who can lead us to the zillofax. I know two others who can show us the way. And so do you."

I pointed to the ground, beyond thumb-sucking Mr. Lester, directly at his two dogs.

chapter twenty-six

Bow-Wow Wow!

"Brutus and Julius know where the zillofax is hidden," I told Vee.

"Dogs cannot talk."

"Maybe not to you or me," I pointed out. "But they can understand my sister. We need Amber's help."

"A human cannot talk to animals."

"She doesn't talk with words. It's like Amber can read their minds. They understand her, too, and do what she wants. Once she got Dribble to ride on a horse and last week she taught her mouse to dive into the bathtub. I don't know how she does it. She just does."

"You are crazy, but I like how you never give up. So I won't give up either." Her hands slipped into her pocket and returned with the bubble-blower tool. "If Amber fails, my rebotco will still take her. I won't be able to stop it."

My heart sagged. "I understand."

Vee held out the najlem and swarms of pink bubbles swirled in the air, a remote control message to the spaceship. It seemed like centuries, but in only two minutes, the rebotco appeared. And there was my sister.

"Amber!" I cried joyfully.

"Cassie? Why are you hugging me?" Amber asked in surprise.

"I'm just glad you're okay!"

"What happened? I was having fun playing." An odd look crept over her face as she glanced down at her hand tucked in her pocket. Then she pointed at Vee. "Cassie, how can I be here and over there?"

Vee still looked like Amber, except for flakey areas of her skin, so it was confusing to see them together.

"Don't ask questions, Amber. Just listen." I checked my watch. "We only have a few minutes. Do you see those dogs?"

Amber nodded. "Poor doggies look sick. Who tied them up? And why is that funny man licking dirt?"

"No questions!" Vee ordered.

"The other me is very bossy," Amber complained.

"Just do as I say, Amber," I said quietly. "The dogs saw that man hide a gold box thing of Vee's. We think it's around here, but we don't know where. Can you help find it?"

Amber was already kneeling on the ground by the dogs and untangling them. They whined, wagged their tails, and gave Amber sloppy, wet kisses. Amber spoke to them softly, scratching behind their ears.

"Amazing," Vee murmured. "How does she do it?"

"I don't know. Vicious monsters turned into gentle dogs. It's like magic."

Amber walked with the dogs. The tamed animals sniffed the ground, circled a fallen tree, and then stopped.

"It's here," Amber called out. "In the broken tree."

Vee rushed to the hollowed tree, peered inside, then shrieked with joy. "My zillofax!" She lifted out a gleaming yellow-gold object that looked like an ordinary, gold suitcase, except for the black straps on each side.

"What does it do?" I asked Vee.

"Nothing."

"Nothing?"

"It's similar to an Earth backpack. I'll show you." She pushed a button, causing the zillofax to pop open, revealing a thick pile of silver paper covered with purple writing.

"This is my homework. Months and months of study," Vee explained, waving the silver paper. "I am so relieved! Now I have the codes to reprogram my rebotco and I won't receive a late penalty from my instructor."

"All you needed were some papers?"

"Yes. The zillofax is merely a container. You can keep it if you want. It's of no importance, like an oyster once you've taken out the pearl. My papers are my pearl."

"Cool! And Amber's free, too." I held tight to my sister's hand.

"I never wasn't free," Amber said as she pulled away, then slipped her hand back into her pocket. "I was playing with my friends."

I shuddered, not wanting to imagine her creepy creature playmates. "Thank goodness you're safe," I told my sister firmly. "Now we can go back to camp."

"And I can return home." Vee smiled at the banana ship which hovered nearby. "I have been away too long."

"But what about him?" I pointed at Mr. Lester who had tugged off one boot and was sucking his big toe. Even as a baby, this guy was a real weirdo!

"He's harmless for a while," Vee assured.

"But that's not enough. He blackmailed my father! And he still has a picture of your spaceship. He has to be punished."

"I will not harm a human."

"That's not what I had in mind." I closed my eyes for a moment and thought hard. What would be a fitting punishment for a thief and blackmailer? My gaze fell on the zillofax, half open and now empty. An oyster with no pearl, yet still useful.

Another one of those fireworks ideas came to me. Shooting stars and bursts of noise rang in my head. *Yes!* It would be true justice in action.

"Vee, did you mean it when you said I could keep the zillofax?" I asked.

"Sure," Vee replied. "But it has no value. The gold is paint and it is recycled from Earth garbage found floating in space. It is no more proof of aliens than the picture Mr. Lester took of my rebotco."

"No proof is the best proof of all!"

"You are so funny, Cassie," Vee remarked. "I shall miss you. Now that it is time to go, I feel sad."

"I'll miss you, too," I admitted. "At least, I hope I will. Are you going to zonk away my memory?"

"I should, but I won't. I trust you to keep my secret, Cassie. But Amber is young and remembering will only upset her." Then, before I could say anything, Vee retrieved her babbzonk and gave Amber a gentle zonk.

Amber blinked like a sleepwalker hearing a sudden noise. She looked around curiously, then slipped her hands in her pockets and turned away from me. I felt guilty, but knew she was better off minus a few memories.

Vee walked to her rebotco. She paused at the doorway and looked back at me. "Thank you for everything. Maybe we will meet again someday. You have been a true friend."

"Goodbye, Vee!" I called out.

"Goodbye, Cassie."

Then she vanished into her spaceship, zooming up into the morning sky.

Vee—my sister, my friend—was gone.

chapter twenty-seven

Just in Time Justice

"Mom! Dad! We're back!" I rang out, running hand in hand with Amber. Except for a quick stop to hide the zillofax in a nearby bush, we'd run all the way back to camp.

"Cassie! Amber! Where have you girls been?" Mom looked up from the ground where she'd been folding her tent. I didn't see Dad, only Lucas, who wore his Sherlock Holmes cloak and seemed to be investigating Dribble's muddy duck prints in the dirt.

Gosh, it was good to be with my family!

Amber ran to Mom with her arms outstretched. "Mommy! Mommy!" She didn't say anything else, just hugged tightly.

"Where have you girls been all morning?"

"I don't know," Amber murmured.

"I left you a note, Mom," I said. "We went on a hike."

"I saw the note, but you should have checked with me first. Why another hike? When did you girls get so interested in exercise?"

"The mountain air gives us lots of energy."

"Save some of that energy for packing." Mom ruffled Amber's curls. "As soon as your father returns and we clean up, we're going home."

"I can't wait!" I exclaimed so enthusiastically that Mom gave me a sharp look.

I still had one important thing to do—and fast! It was after noon, and Mr. Lester's press conference would begin soon.

Fifteen minutes later, the picnic table was cleaned off and the garbage was picked up. Sleeping bags were rolled neatly. And I had hidden the zillofax in a very secret place.

Dust churned up on the road as TV-news crews paraded into camp in cars, vans, and trucks. I noticed one of the vans had the *Mooncroft's Miracles* logo on the side. But only Dad's show would have the whole story. Dad, Ms. Dumano, and cameraman Fred already had equipment set up near Mr. Lester's campsite.

Mom, Lucas, and Amber (with Dribble trailing behind her) headed to watch the show, too. Smiling, I assured Mom there would definitely be a show to watch.

To everyone's surprise (except mine) Mr. Lester didn't show up. The eager crowd grew restless, and by 1:15 whispers and rumors spread like a wildfire. At 1:30, Mooncroft's crew grumbled that this was a "wild goose chase," then they drove away. By two o'clock, Dad's *I Don't Believe It!* crew was the only media remaining. But even they were ready to give up.

"Dad!" I begged when Dad told cameraman Fred to put away his equipment. "Wait a little longer."

"For what? I knew Mr. Lester was a crook and this proves it even more." Dad turned to speak quietly to Ms. Dumano, and my spirits sank.

Time for Plan B.

"Dad!" I exclaimed so loud everyone turned to stare at me, which normally would make me embarrassed, but now it made me proud. A seeker of truth, that's what Vee called me.

"What is it, Cassie?" Dad asked in a tired voice.

"Since you're here, why not do more investigating?" I gestured to Mr. Lester's camp. "You never know what you might find."

"It would only be another waste of time," Dad scoffed, tipping up his sunglasses.

"But it can't hurt to try," I insisted.

"She has a point, Jon," Ms. Dumano said. "Let's poke around a bit."

"I'll keep the tape running." Fred grinned. "Could be, maybe, might be interesting."

They looked under the table, behind the trailer, around the truck . . . and finally they neared the doghouses. Ms. Dumano tip-toed carefully around the dirty cages in her spikey, black high heels.

"Jon! Look at this!" Ms. Dumano squealed, bending down and peering into the doghouse. "We've struck paydirt!" I was amazed as she dropped to her knees—designer skirt and all!—— reached into the doghouse. "There's a gold box of some kind hidden in here!"

"Yes!" I pumped my fist, as Dad strode over to Ms. Dumano to get a better look.

"Hold it right there!" a deep voice hollered. "That gold thingamajig's mine!"

We all whirled around and there was Mr. Lester.

His expression was fierce as a pack of rabid dogs. I definitely liked him better when he was drooling and sucking his big toe. But all little babies have to grow up eventually.

"This is my camp and my alien thing!" Mr. Lester shoved through the small crowd and snatched the zillofax from Ms. Dumano. "No one gets this without paying me first."

"Where have you been, Lester?" Dad demanded. "News crews waited over an hour for you. You're lucky I'm still here."

"I— I musta bumped my head in the woods." He rubbed his forehead and blinked with confusion. "It was danged weird. I can't remember much and then when I called my dogs, they just ran from me. Anyhow, that gold thingamajig is mine, Strange. It's from an alien spaceship and it's going to make me rich."

"Rich?" Dad shared an amused glance with Ms. Dumano. "I don't think so, Lester. No one won't listen to you now—not even that swindler Mooncroft. How can you prove that gold box came from space? Anyone can paint a metal box gold."

"Look at it for yourself!" Lester barked, shoving the zillofax into Dad's hands.

"Sure, thing." Dad winked at Fred. The cameraman winked back. "It *is* unusual," Dad commented, rubbing his hands over the zillofax. "Hmmm . . . what's this button?"

Dad sprung the release and the zillofax popped open. Only instead of alien silver papers, dozens of pinecones rained out, falling on the ground.

"Pinecones!" everyone exclaimed.

"It's a fake!" Dad proclaimed.

I couldn't hold back my laughter anymore. I doubled over and cracked up. At last! A practical use for pinecones!

Everyone went kind of crazy after that. Mr. Lester had a grown-up tantrum: stomped his feet, turned red in the face, and yelled a lot. He started arguing and shouting at everyone. Finally, he stormed into his trailer and slammed the door.

Then with cameras rolling, my father spoke his famous words that would be heard on national TV next week: "Another fraud exposed. A phony photograph of a spaceship. A painted gold box full of pinecones. And now you know why *I don't believe it!*"

I applauded. All right, Dad!

Since no one was paying any attention to the zillofax anymore, I grabbed it and headed back to camp. I hid the zillofax under my seat in the van. It was my gift from Vee, and I would treasure it always.

What a campout! I thought, sitting at the picnic table and breathing fresh mountain air. A kidnapped sister, a spaceship, pink bubbles, doodlezapps, and an out-of-this-world friend. Dad would prove to his viewing audience that aliens did not exist. Only I would know the true story.

I looked at the spot of shining blue still shimmering on my fingertip. In a few days, the blue would fade and vanish. But my memories of Vee would stay with me always.

Would I ever see her again?

A giggle from my tent jolted me from my thoughts.

Creeping over, I heard Amber whisper, "Don't tickle me!"

I figured she was playing a new game with Dribble. Only when I peeked through a mesh window, the duck wasn't there. Amber was completely alone. But I swear I saw something wiggle in her pocket.

What was my sister up to now?

Win a free book!

So, what is Amber up to now?

Send us your best guess about what's wiggling in Amber's pocket by January 1, 2005, and we'll pass it along to Linda Joy Singleton. She'll pick ten lucky winners who will receive a free book from Llewellyn. Send your guesses and the completed permission form on the next page to:

Llewellyn Publications
Attn: Megan, Acquisitions
P.O. Box 64383
St. Paul, MN 55164-0383 USA

Rules and Entry Form

1. Deadline for entry is January 1, 2005.
2. Must be 16 or younger to enter.
3. One guess per entry, and one entry per eligible person.
4. No Llewellyn employees or their family members may enter.
5. All entries must have parental permission (see form below).

Name: _____

Address: _____

_____

E-mail: _____

Age: _____

Guess: _____

_____

I, _____, (parent/legal guardian) give my son/daughter, _____, express permission to enter this contest. I also give Llewellyn Publications express permission to send any materials to my son/daughter should s/he be the winner of this contest.

Signed: _____ Date: _____

Find the answer in

Shamrocked!

by
Linda Joy Singleton

Coming in January 2005
The second book in the Strange Encounters series
from Llewellyn Publications.

DIADEM WORLDS OF MAGIC

A New Series by John Peel from Llewellyn Publications

Score is young street rat from New York City. Helaine is a fierce girl-warrior from the planet Ordin. Pixel is a Virtual Reality junkie from the planet Calomir. All from different worlds, these seemingly ordinary kids are brought by some unseen force to the Diadem, a mutlilayered magical universe, where they must rely on their own growing arsenal of magical skills and each other to survive danger and to discover just who has brought them here, and why.

Book of Names

The first book of the series tells how Score, Helaine, and Pixel begin their journey to the center of the Diadem. On the planet Treen they encounter three magical, shapeshifting Beastials, angry mobs, and a mysterious wizard, who might be out to help them reach their magical potential—or to destroy them and take it for himself.

ISBN 0-7387-0617-5 $4.99